27 March 1982 - Strandson & ...

2cc

A House Full of Echoes

ALSO BY MARA KAY

In Face of Danger

A HOUSE FULL OF ECHOES

by Mara Kay

CROWN PUBLISHERS, INC.   NEW YORK

Published in the United States in 1981
Copyright © 1980 by Mara Kay
Published in Great Britain in 1980 under the title *Restless Shadows.*
Manufactured in the United States of America
Published simultaneously in Canada by General Publishing Company Limited
10 9 8 7 6 5 4 3 2 1

The text of this book is set in 11/15 Palatino.

Library of Congress Cataloging in Publication Data
Kay, Mara.
A house full of echoes.
Previously published as: Restless shadows. 1980.
Summary: When Astrovo, a once-splendid
country estate, is turned into a finishing school,
the spirits of former inhabitants seek to reenact their lives.
[1. Ghost stories] I. Title. PZ7. K198Ho 1981
AACR2 ISBN 0-517-54422-9 [Fic] 81-4094

CONTENTS

A House Full of Echoes

1

The New Venture

A family council was to take place in the library of Astrovo at six o'clock in the evening. Malvina, as the elder daughter of the house, had decreed it and no one would have dared to dispute her order.

At a quarter to six, Lavrentii, the only one left of what had once been an army of footmen, painfully climbed on a chair and lit the two candelabras standing on the mantelpiece in front of the big, bronze-framed mirror. It was not an easy task; the candles were used so rarely that the wicks had become dry and shriveled. The old man waited patiently for the flames to take hold while scraping drops of wax off the marble and carefully avoiding looking in the mirror.

When the little red tongues of flame ceased to hiss and shot upward, quivering in the draft coming from the windows, Lavrentii sighed with satisfaction and began to descend from his perch. One foot on the floor, he hesitated, then peeked in the mirror. He shrank back, muttering, "Heaven be with us."

Still mumbling under his breath, he shuffled across the room and drew together the window drapes of faded purple velvet. Once the dark February evening was shut out, the library became cozier, even warmer, in spite of the rather meager fire burning in the fireplace. Faint traces of embossed gold gleamed on the leather upholstery of the armchairs, and the garlands of flowers on the rug looked mellow instead of merely shabby.

Producing a small feather duster from the deep pocket of his livery, Lavrentii flicked it over the big, carved oak table standing in the middle of the room and over the glass doors of the bookcases lining the walls. Bending down, he contemplated the curls of dust clinging to the rug. These needed sweeping up, but he decided that in the candlelight no one would notice. There was no time anyway. The tall redwood door opened, and two men entered.

The one in front walked heavily, leaning on a silver-topped cane. His ruddy face, under a mane of white hair, twitched with pain at every step. His companion sauntered along lightly on long legs made even longer by tight white breeches. "How do you feel, Nicolas?" he kept asking anxiously. "Would you like to take my arm?"

The man with the cane waved him aside. "Please let me be, Erast." He sank into the armchair hastily pushed forward by Lavrentii. "Thunder and lightning," he grumbled, loosening the lace scarf at his throat. "Just a few steps, and I'm out of breath. Old age tells."

"Don't you talk like that. You are not old," Lavrentii contradicted, bringing a footstool.

"Sixty-seven last October. That is old enough, Lavrentii, and gout does not help. Ah, this is better. . . ." Nicolas extended one foot in an old-fashioned buckled shoe on the footstool and placed his cane on the floor beside it.

Lavrentii's small, red-lidded eyes stared first at Nicolas, then at Erast, sitting on the edge of his chair and nervously watching the door. Strange how two brothers could be so different, the old footman thought. Erast was not young either, but while Nicolas looked like an aging lion, Erast resembled an old woman with his long, anxious face. Now he was waiting for his half sister to appear. Always was afraid of her, from the time they were children. . . . Oh! Lavrentii gulped and stood at attention.

Sharp heels tap-tapped behind the door, and Malvina Astrova came in. Very tall and thin, in a high-waisted yellow gown that cast a sallow tinge over her face, she stood on the threshold, pulling a small black shawl tighter over her shoulders. "Lavrentii, it is cold in here. Please build up the fire."

Somewhere along his half-century of service, Lavrentii had lost the habit of addressing his masters as *barin* or *barinia*. He grumbled, "No wood. Got right down to the chalk mark."

At these last words, Nicolas, who was taking a pinch of tobacco out of a leather pouch for his pipe, looked up with a jerk. "Chalk mark? What is he talking about?"

Going to the fireplace, Malvina held out her hands to the barely flickering flame. "It means that wood is being so wastefully used all over the house, and especially in the kitchen"—she glanced at Lavrentii—"that I was obliged to go to the shed and put chalk marks on the wall by the woodpile. Now the servants know exactly how much wood they can take out every day."

Nicolas gave a bark of laughter. "I see. How very ingenious!"

"But why go to such extremes?" Erast said in a shocked voice. "Surely we could have a few trees cut down. After all, we still own part of the woods."

His brother gave another guffaw. "Cut down trees instead of buying wood from peasants? Who is going to do the cutting? All our serfs have been sold or died of old age, and the hired servants are above that kind of work. Perhaps Lavrentii here could try. Eh, Lavrentii?"

Erast sighed. "Maybe we should not have sold the entire village, but it did seem more humane not to separate families."

"It also brought us more money," Malvina declared, "and money is exactly what I want to talk to all of you about this evening." She looked around. "Vanda is late, as usual."

Erast said quietly, "She is still grieving for her fiancé. It makes her forget the time."

"After thirty years!" Malvina took a poker and prodded the smoldering log viciously. "She was not even engaged to that man. He was only courting her. And the interesting part is, she intended to refuse him! It was only after he fell off a horse and was killed that she became his grieving bride. I wonder if she still remembers his name."

"Ahem." Erast coughed warningly as the door opened and Vanda came into the room.

"Really, sister!" Malvina exclaimed, gazing severely at the short, plump figure wrapped in a white lace shawl over a white dimity dress sprigged with violets. "Summer clothes in this weather!"

Vanda's round blue eyes looked piteously at Malvina. She stood in the middle of the floor fingering her light draperies. "But I just wanted to wear something pretty," she murmured. "We so seldom go visiting, I never have an occasion to dress nicely, and I am tired of all those dark winter things. This *is* a gathering and I thought. . . ."

Malvina nodded. "You are right, Vanda. This is a gathering . . . of a kind. Never mind, please sit down. Mademoiselle is not here yet."

Nicolas raised his eyebrows. "Mademoiselle? What do you need her for? She is deaf, and most of the time she doesn't even know what is going on around her."

"She can hear very well when she chooses," Malvina said, "and she is not *that* vague. Ah, here she comes." An elderly woman, almost bent in two and wrapped in something gray and shapeless, shuffled in. Erast immediately jumped up and led her to a chair.

Mademoiselle's sharp, birdlike eyes darted around. "What is it? What is it?" she asked, tucking stray hairs under her white bonnet. "Why are you all here? Who has died?"

"No one has died, Mademoiselle. We are simply going to discuss certain matters," Malvina told her. "You brought up Vanda and me, and after all these years we consider you a member of the family." She suddenly turned and looked over her shoulder. "Are you still here, Lavrentii?"

The old footman bristled. "Yes, I am. I know that no one needs me when there is no work to be done, but when you started to talk about money, I thought I might as well stay. After all, it concerns me too."

Malvina frowned, but Nicolas said, "Let him stay. Really, Malvina, if I had known you assembled us all here to tell us we are ruined, I would not have bothered to come."

Erast leaned forward, twisting his fingers. "My apiary is be-ginning to bring in some income, Malvina. The honey we sold last summer. . . ." His mild, shortsighted eyes met his half sister's snapping black ones, and he stopped in midsentence.

"It will take much more honey just to pay for that glass beehive you bought recently, dear brother," Malvina said bitterly. She shook her head. "Really, Erast, sometimes I fail to understand you! A drunken sailor knocks on our back door and asks for permission to sleep in our hayloft. You spend an entire evening talking to him, and on the strength of some wild story, you take a trip to Odessa, across half of Russia! Knowing how much we need every penny."

"But, Malvina—"

"You bring home some half-dead bees," she continued, "and you buy an expensive glass beehive, *on credit,* in order to watch them."

"Malvina, please listen to me." Erast began to twist his fingers harder. "That sailor *did* see a very special kind of bee in Africa. He told me about it and offered to bring me a swarm from his next voyage there. But he had no more leave, so I *had* to meet him in Odessa seaport. He kept his promise even though only a few bees survived. Luckily, the queen was among them. They are multiplying rapidly, and after a few experiments. . . ."

"Let's simply sell another parcel of land," Nicolas suggested. "The money will keep our creditors quiet for a while."

Vanda's small, fluttering hand appeared from the depths of her armchair. "Not the park! We can't sell the park, Nicolas, and there is no other land left."

"Well, then. . . ." Nicolas brushed specks of tobacco off his lapels. "If the situation is really so bad, why not sell the entire estate? Even after paying all the debts there should be enough left for us to settle somewhere abroad—in Italy, maybe. The climate would be excellent for my gout."

"We shall never sell Astrovo! At least, not while I am alive." Malvina threw back her head and waited for protests.

None came. Erast exclaimed helplessly, "But what are we going to do if there is no way of raising money!"

For the first time that evening, Malvina smiled. "Yes, there is. You all seem to have forgotten that Ada is coming home in March. She has completed her studies and must take only a few more examinations to obtain her diploma."

Nicolas snorted. "Diploma! From that little *pensionnat* in Tula."

Malvina pursed her lips. "It is an excellent school, and it is fortunate we could scrape enough money together to send her there. Otherwise, lessons with Mademoiselle would have been the beginning and the end of her education."

Malvina had lowered her voice for the last sentence, but Mademoiselle heard it. Sitting up, the gray hairs on her chin trembling, she glared at everyone in turn. "Heartless, heartless!" she moaned. "After all the trouble I took to teach that child . . ."

"We know it, Mademoiselle, and we are grateful," Malvina said quickly. "I did not mean to offend you."

Nicolas said, "Niece Ada . . . you know, I almost forgot her existence. Even when she is at home, one hardly notices her. Yet she was a lively enough child when I brought her from Warsaw in . . . let's see . . . in 1806. I wonder if her upbringing was not too austere. I seem to remember children's parties and dancing lessons planned for her. But nothing like that ever took place."

"Of course not!" Malvina's voice became shrill. "When we first learned that Ada's parents had died in an accident and that she was coming to live with us, I expected her to be well provided for. But when it turned out that she was destitute, I had to change my plans. I made Ada realize that she could not indulge in any whims or fantasies, and that it was her duty to repay us with obedience and industry for giving her a home."

"Perhaps that is what made her look like a little old lady instead of a child," Nicolas mumbled.

"She was afraid, too," Vanda put in quietly.

Erast started. "Afraid? Of what? Oh, I see. . . ."

There was a long and heavy silence. At last Erast said, "But what about Ada? How is her diploma supposed to help us?"

"Yes," Nicolas added, "just how is Ada going to save us from being ruined, Malvina? Are you hoping for a rich marriage? She is not a beauty."

"Oh, I don't know," Vanda protested. "I think she is very attractive."

As if to settle the dispute, Lavrentii picked up one of the candelabras. A painting, hanging on the wall beside the fireplace, swam out of the darkness. Two black, slightly slanted eyes set in a heart-shaped, very white face stared indifferently from the canvas. The dark hair was parted in the middle and woven into tight little curls at the temples. Narrow, still childish shoulders rose from a low-necked wine-colored gown.

"How old is she in that painting?" Erast asked. "About fifteen?"

Malvina answered, "Yes, just about."

Another long silence followed. Finally Nicolas ordered, "Put it down, man. We have admired niece Ada long enough. Not a bad effort on the part of her drawing master, and I must admit that there is character in her face. However, as I said before, she is not a beauty."

Malvina shrugged. "For a teaching position, beauty is not necessary."

"Teaching!" Erast exclaimed. "You are going to send that poor child, barely eighteen, to be a governess in a stranger's home?"

"Not at all. She is going to teach right here, in this library. My plan is"—Malvina paused dramatically— "to open a boarding school at Astrovo."

"*What!*" Forgetting his bad leg, Nicolas got up from his seat, swore, and collapsed again, almost upsetting the footstool.

Erast and Vanda started to speak, interrupting each other. Malvina raised her hand. "Kindly let me explain. All over the county of Tula there are wealthy landowners who cannot bear the idea of sending their daughters away to school, or even of having a governess, a stranger, in their house."

Erast murmured, a dazed look in his eyes, "But what makes you think the parents would elect to send their daughters to us?"

"Because they would prefer a *family* to a real boarding school," his half sister answered decisively. "We will charge a considerable fee to impress them. Ada's *pensionnat* charges four hundred rubles in silver per year. We will charge five hundred. I think six pupils will be enough to start with."

Vanda stared around her, looking completely bewildered. "But how are we going to get them?"

Malvina smiled triumphantly. "I have written a few letters, and we have one pupil already. The Countess de Gramont wishes us to take her granddaughter, Marguerite."

"Countess de Gramont?" Nicolas seemed sincerely surprised. "Is that why she paid us a visit some time ago? But if I am not mistaken, her granddaughter attended Ada's *pensionnat* for a short time, but the countess took her away. So why send her here?"

Malvina dismissed his objection. "That was a long time ago.

The child was probably too young for school. She is sixteen now."

"Well, well," Nicolas muttered, leaning back in his chair. "At least the countess can afford our outrageous fee. Lost everything in the French Revolution, came to Russia practically a pauper, and now she is one of the richest women in the county. Was never above dabbling in trade."

"That is why *her* estate is not mortgaged," Malvina retorted. "Talking about trade, we may have another pupil—Irina Makarova. Her father owns a hardware store in Tula."

Nicolas frowned. "I think I heard someone mention recently that Makarov inherited a large sum of money on the death of his godfather. So now he wants his daughter to be brought up in a grand style. Ha, ha!"

Erast shook his head. "I'm afraid I still do not quite understand. What is Ada going to teach these girls?"

"You mean, what are *we* going to teach them?" Malvina's eyes narrowed as she surveyed each member of the family in turn.

"We?" Erast shrank back. "What could I possibly teach them?"

"Botany. Just take them around the grounds and talk about trees and flowers. Or talk about insects—your bees, for instance. You, Vanda, can teach needlework and supply music for the dancing lessons."

"Oh, I couldn't! I mean, I don't mind teaching needlework, I know so many beautiful stitches, but music . . . no. My grief—"

Mademoiselle saw Malvina's eyes move in her direction. "No and no!" she shrilled, punctuating every word with a slap on the arm of her chair. "I am not going to teach little children the French alphabet. I am too old for that."

Malvina sighed. "There will be no small children,

Mademoiselle. Our school will be for young ladies. I was only going to ask you to pretend you don't understand Russian when they talk to you. This will make them address you in French."

Mademoiselle considered the matter for a moment. "Yes, I could do that, and if they don't know French, they will leave me alone."

"May I inquire if I am to have the honor of being a preceptor too?" Nicolas asked.

Malvina ignored his sarcasm. "Certainly. You can teach history and geography. I had the old globe cleaned and brought down from the attic." She threw back her shoulders and smoothed her shawl. "I am going to teach deportment. As soon as it gets warmer, I will have the old blue carriage brought from the stables and placed by the back porch."

"The old blue carriage," Erast repeated. "Whatever for? It is completely broken down."

His half sister eyed him with disdain. "I am not planning to use it for driving. The pupils are going to practice how to get in and out of a carriage gracefully. That is important. As for Ada, she can teach French and German literature, the art of writing letters, music, and dancing."

Nicolas cleared his throat. "I trust that all this . . . er . . . madness is not going to take place till autumn?"

"It is going to take place the first week of April."

"But," Vanda said, "summer is supposed to be a time for holidays."

"Oh, my goodness!" Malvina exclaimed, exasperated. "Don't you all realize that in late autumn the roads become impassable? Besides, in the country, people start to get ready for Christmas in November and go on celebrating into January. Most parents would never let their daughters be away from home at that time. Anyway, we could not afford to heat the house properly. The best plan for us is to start in April and close by the first of November."

Nicolas began to heave himself up. "Since we have only about six weeks' respite, I am going to begin by taking a good rest in my room. Help me, Lavrentii."

Vanda got up too. "I think I have a headache. A vinegar compress may help."

Erast helped Mademoiselle to rise and, taking her arm, led her to the door. Malvina watched them go. As Nicolas passed her, he asked with a grin, "Just one more question, my dear. How are *they* going to feel about our having all those strangers under our roof?"

Malvina adjusted her shawl. *"They* never bothered me, and I can say the same for Ada."

Nicolas gave her a long look. "You, yes. But I wouldn't be so sure about Ada." Changing his tone, he said abruptly, "May I take your arm, so Lavrentii can put out the lights?"

A few minutes later, the library was dark and silent. Then came whispers, faint laughter, and the rustle of skirts. A giant crystal chandelier, ablaze with lights, appeared in the mirror. Its candles flickered, then went out, one by one.

2

Marguerite

"You do understand why I want you to go to that school at Astrovo, Marguerite?"

The Countess de Gramont and her granddaughter were sitting in the corner room, which the countess especially liked because it received even more sunshine than the rest of the house. Sunbeams were pouring now through two open windows, making a halo around Marguerite's chestnut head as she sat perched on the windowsill, and sparkling upon the knitting needles in her grandmother's hands.

At the countess's question, Marguerite swung around. "No, grandmaman, I don't really understand. You did not want me to stay in that *pensionnat* in Tula, so why do you want to send me away now? I am so happy here with you."

The countess laid down her knitting, and her sunken gray eyes looked at Marguerite across the room. "I took you out of that *pensionnat* because you were only learning bits of subjects, nothing in depth. Your education was too important to me. So I tried to teach you myself, and now you know much more than most girls of your age, even though I had to box your ears sometimes for not paying attention. At that time, however, you were quite content to play with the gardener's daughters and the coachman's niece. Now you are sixteen. You need the companionship of girls who read the same books as you do, and who are brought up in the same way. We are too far from other estates to have guests often, and when we go visiting, you just sit in a corner and say nothing."

"I like to watch people better than talk to them."

"Perhaps, but it is also because you are so used to being alone. When your brother leaves for Heidelberg University in October, you will be quite lonely. Well, those are the reasons I want you to go to Astrovo. But mind"—the countess raised her finger—"if you are not happy there, let me know immediately. A messenger on horseback will be coming every week to bring you my letters and to pick up yours."

Marguerite's small, round face remained grave. "I understand now, grandmaman, but I am still a little frightened. All those strangers! I only know Ada. She was at the *pensionnat* too. She has many uncles and aunts, doesn't she?"

"Not really. The late Mr. Astrov was married twice. The two brothers, Nicolas and Erast, are from his first marriage. When he became a widower, he married a Polish lady and had two daughters, Malvina and Vanda, both spinsters. That is all."

Marguerite looked puzzled. "Whose daughter is Ada?"

"Oh, Nicolas and Erast had an older sister, Olga. She died a long time ago. Ada is her granddaughter."

Marguerite murmured, "Yes, grandmaman."

The countess went on, "I visited Astrovo recently, and I have no doubt you will be comfortable there. Everything is shabby but clean, and the house is still decent even though it is so neglected. A pity, it used to be very beautiful."

"Like the chateau de Gramont in France, grandmaman?"

"One cannot compare them. Astrovo is just a country house, barely a hundred years old. Parts of the chateau de Gramont date back to the Crusades. The priest of Gramont village wrote to me last year. He thought I should come back and visit, but I replied that he should not expect me." She paused. "When I crossed the Russian border, I promised myself to forget the past and make a new life for myself and my son, and I have kept my word."

Marguerite did not answer. She was thinking about the story of how her grandfather had been taken prisoner by the revolutionaries and guillotined, and how the family of the Russian ambassador in Paris had helped her grandmother escape. They had disguised her as their maid and passed off her ten-year-old son, Marguerite's father, as one of their children.

With a sigh, she came back to the present and realized that her grandmother was still talking to her.

"I had a few pieces of jewelry with me," the countess was saying. "Earrings and a couple of bracelets. I hid them in my hair. Luckily, in those times ladies wore their hair piled high, so the revolutionary guards who inspected the carriage never found them. When we arrived in Russia I stayed with the ambassador's family for a little while, then started to look for a house I could call my own. Only I did not have enough money for a house. Then someone offered me a barn with some land around it. The price was low, so I bought it. This house was a barn once." The countess began to laugh. "Of course, I tried to make it pleasant and comfortable, but never luxurious. Barns and luxury don't go together. So we have barefooted maids instead of footmen, and chintzes instead of brocades."

The countess leaned back and half-closed her eyes. "It took time and energy," she said. "I spent many a sleepless night, poring over the account books, but I am proud of what I have achieved."

"Yes, indeed, grandmaman," Marguerite said, thinking of the big dairy, the weaving room where several girls sat at their looms, the sewing room where the homemade fabric was cut and turned into garments, sheets, or tablecloths, the wagons loaded with poultry and vegetables that were constantly sent to the market in Tula.

"I only wish your parents were alive and with us," the countess murmured. She suddenly straightened up and went on in her usual firm voice. "Let's look at the list of things you are to take with you. Hand me that sheet of paper on the top of the secretary."

"Here, grandmaman."

"Hm . . ." Her grandmother took up the lorgnette hanging around her neck on a black velvet ribbon, and began to study the list. "What is this?" She peered closer. "Oh, I see! You were supposed to leave early in April, so I included a warm cloak and two wool gowns, but you kept coughing so long after that bad cold. . . . We can leave these things out; you won't need them in the middle of May. Now listen while I read the list to you, and remind me if I have forgotten anything.

"Six white sarcenet petticoats, one yellow silk petticoat—you can wear it under that white net dress—three pairs of striped stockings, one pair . . . Marguerite! Are you listening? My goodness, don't lean so far out or you'll fall. What is so interesting in the garden?"

Marguerite jerked herself back. "I was looking at the white rosebush, grandmaman. It is going to be in bloom soon."

"Nonsense! One does not wave to a rosebush."

16

Rising swiftly, the countess went to the window and called, "Gaston!"

The hedge of lilac separating the flower garden from the kitchen wing parted and a young man stepped out. Slim and long-legged, in white nankeen trousers and blue jacket, he had Marguerite's brown, wavy hair and brown eyes. Higher cheekbones and a stubborn jaw made him resemble his grandmother.

He inquired politely, "Did you want me, grandmaman?"

"No, but I do want you to keep out of the kitchen. The cook is busy. I have ordered lunch early so that you and your sister can leave about two. I think you should go to the stables and make sure Vlas is not getting drunk. I ordered the small coach; it's lighter and the roads are still bad."

"Certainly, grandmaman." Gaston turned and vanished into the lilacs again.

Standing on tiptoe and watching over her grandmother's shoulder, Marguerite spied a large wicker basket hidden among the bushes. Trust Gaston not to be caught, she thought admiringly.

Returning to her chair, the countess picked up her lorgnette again. "The trouble is, you are too serious and your brother is too scatterbrained." She smoothed out the list of Marguerite's wardrobe. "Listen now! One velvet cape with hood . . ."

"Yes, grandmaman," Marguerite murmured.

3

The Picnic

The parting was over. Sitting in the coach beside her brother, Marguerite watched the green roof of the house disappear behind the trees. She had done her best not to cry, but when she saw her two trunks being strapped to the roof of the coach, she broke down and threw herself, sobbing, into her grandmother's arms. The countess hugged Marguerite tightly. "May God keep you safe, darling child. I will see you in November when you come home, full of stories about your life at Astrovo."

How *was* it going to be at Astrovo? Marguerite swallowed her tears and began to feel the first pricks of curiosity. How would the other girls be dressed, for instance? Settling back, she smoothed the skirt of her new green traveling gown. The sewing maid had followed exactly the illustration in *La Mode* magazine, which came from Paris every month. There was a stiff ruffle around the throat, and three more ruffles ornamented the ankle-length skirt. The sash was almost under the armpits and was tied in a big bow with streamers at the back.

Taking a small hand mirror from her green velvet reticule, Marguerite made sure that her bonnet of white straw fitted gracefully, retied the white ribbons under her chin, and felt much better. Closing the bag with a snap, she put it on her lap and looked up at her brother. His expression was grave.

"Gaston," she whispered. "Are we really going to have it?"

Turning his head with difficulty because of the high collar almost reaching his ears, Gaston looked at Marguerite with vague eyes. Suddenly, his face cleared and he winked at her. "Our picnic, you mean? Of course. The basket is under the seat, and you should see the food the cook gave me!"

Marguerite clapped her hands. "Oh, how wonderful! But . . . perhaps we should have asked grandmaman's permission."

"She would never permit it! I am escorting you to school, which is a serious business. Besides, it's more fun this way, and we are only going to stop for about half an hour, so where's the harm?"

"What about Vlas? He might tell grandmaman."

"He won't. I have something that will keep him quiet."

Marguerite sighed contentedly, and sniffed at the air coming through the open coach window. They were just entering the woods, which smelled of pine, moss, and warm earth spiced by a strong whiff of horses' sweat. It was almost too warm for May.

Gaston was fanning himself with his handkerchief. Suddenly he continued, "And if our picnic makes us late, all the better. Time enough for you to arrive at that place."

Marguerite kept silent. At last she said slowly, "You don't really want me to go to Astrovo, I can tell. Why?"

Her brother frowned. "Why? Well, I've heard some strange stories about that family. Most of them are probably idle tales, but one I do believe."

Marguerite sat up. "Really? Do tell me. Please."

"I suppose I might as well. I heard it about two years ago, from a classmate of mine. His parents went on a long trip abroad, so he spent his summer vacation with some relatives near Tula. They were old people and he was terribly bored, so he went for long rides on horseback. One day he went farther than usual and lost his way. Evening came, and to make matters worse it started to rain. My friend was getting tired and a little scared, so he was delighted when he suddenly emerged into a long avenue that led him to a house. It was quite dark by then, but he still could see that the house was big and beautiful and that in front of it was a magnificent rose garden and a marble fountain with a statue in the middle of it. He knocked on the door and introduced himself. The owners of the house turned out to be the Astrovs. They were very gracious and invited him to spend the night."

"What happened to him?" Marguerite asked.

"Nothing happened to him. But when he woke up in the morning and looked out of the window, all he could see in front of the house was a badly mown plot of grass with a few mossy stones in the middle that *could* once have been a fountain."

"I—I don't understand." Marguerite faltered. "Did your friend *dream* about that rose garden?"

"He swears he didn't, and I believe him. He is not the kind that makes up stories."

They were leaving the woods. The trees thinned into groves. Then meadows rolled by, the green grass rippling in the breeze.

Gaston thrust his head out of the window and began to give

directions to the coachman. The coach turned heavily into a side road with small tufts of grass growing in the deep ruts. "A river!" Marguerite exclaimed, as a sheet of water appeared from behind a group of trees.

"It's the Oka. We are there."

"Thank goodness." Marguerite clung to her seat as the coach bounced over the ruts. Another jerk, and it stopped.

Gaston opened the door and jumped out. Marguerite gathered up her skirts and jumped out too, ignoring her brother's hand. "How lovely," she said, looking at two giant oaks growing side by side on a green slope rolling down to the river. "How did you find this place?"

"Just stumbled on it while riding some time ago. What is Vlas grumbling about?"

"I think he doesn't approve of our stopping here," Marguerite answered, glancing at the coachman clambering down from his high seat.

"Never mind. He'll change his tune when he sees what I have for him. Just let me get the basket."

"Tell Vlas not to unharness the horses. We can't stay too long," Marguerite called over her shoulder as she ran to the water's edge.

It was so warm, she was tempted to take off her shoes and stockings and wade in but changed her mind as she realized the water was not as shallow as it looked. Shading her eyes, she gazed at a small black cloud on the horizon. It seemed out of place in the immense expanse of blue sky. Could it mean rain? It did not seem likely. The cloud was too small and too far away.

"Marguerite, come! Everything is ready." She clambered up the slope.

A blue tablecloth, somewhat frayed at the edges, was spread

on the grass and covered with dishes. Marguerite clasped her hands. "A roasted chicken, ham, and an apple tart! How did you manage to get all that food?"

"The cook likes me. She says I am the finest young man in the entire county of Tula," Gaston explained, rummaging in the basket. "But she could only provide these." He took out a few tin plates and kitchen forks and knives. "I did not dare to ask the housekeeper for silver, but I did manage to get these." He pointed at two small silver goblets.

Marguerite laughed. "What are we going to drink out of these? Water from the river?"

"This!" Her brother thrust his hand into the basket again and pulled out a bottle.

"Grandmaman's *nalivka!*" Marguerite gasped. "Let me see the label. Why, it is old. You must have taken it from that special shelf."

"I don't remember which shelf it was. I just snatched the bottle nearest the cellar door."

"It is probably strong," Marguerite murmured, eyeing the bottle with misgiving. Every summer she helped the house-keeper fill several wide-mouthed bottles with ripe cherries. Then sugar was added and the bottles were arranged in a neat row on the sunny windowsill of the pantry. When the juice started to ferment, the countess took over, straining, measuring, and adding alcohol. The discarded cherries were candied and used for desserts. *Nalivka* was served only when there were guests, and Marguerite was allowed a thimbleful.

"I don't think we should drink it," she declared, putting the bottle down. "It seems a wicked thing to do."

"Wicked! You sound as if we were going to get drunk," her brother said indignantly. "We are only going to take a sip. The rest is for Vlas."

"Almost a whole bottle! That is too much."

"Not for him. He is used to vodka, which is much stronger. And now"—Gaston filled the goblets and handed one to Marguerite—"let's drink to your happiness and success at Astrovo!"

At the name of Astrovo, Marguerite's smile faded. She put down her glass and asked, "Gaston, did you tell grandmaman your classmate's story?"

He nodded soberly. "Yes, I did, and got a long lecture about this being the year of our Lord 1818 and not the Middle Ages. She may be right after all. Let's forget it. To your good health!"

He drained his goblet, and Marguerite did the same.

"Excellent. Grandmaman knows how to make *nalivka*. Let's have another one."

Marguerite drank her second goblet slowly, expecting to feel dizzy. Instead she only felt hungry and reached for some ham. She munched contentedly while Gaston took the rest of the *nalivka* and a plate of food to Vlas.

The coachman accepted the bottle suspiciously and muttered something about the *barinia* having ordered him to drive to Astrovo, not to risk the horses' legs on godforsaken roads.

"He doesn't seem to be impressed by *nalivka*," Marguerite commented when her brother came back.

"Don't worry, he will be after the first sip." Gaston settled down on the grass. "Pass me the chicken, please."

When the dishes were empty, Marguerite murmured regretfully, "I suppose we shall have to leave soon."

Gaston glanced over his shoulder. "I don't think Vlas is ready to leave yet," he whispered. Marguerite followed his gaze. The coachman was asleep on his back, his mouth open, the empty bottle beside him.

An hour ago, this sight would have filled Marguerite with dismay, but now she felt too comfortable to worry about it.

"Let him sleep a while," she suggested airily. Her brother leaned against the oak and closed his eyes. "I will rest too. Just for a minute," Marguerite murmured, stretching herself on the blanket, her head in the crook of her arm.

The next thing she knew, she was in a boat, floating down the Oka. Big flocks of strange white birds were flying around, almost touching her with their wings. She tried to chase them away, but they pressed closer. At last the largest bird flew into her face.

Marguerite woke up and screamed. There *was* something flapping against her face. She snatched at it and saw that it was the tablecloth. All around, everything seemed to be flying. Leaves, bits of wood and grass, even small branches were whirling in the air. Gaston suddenly came into sight, careering wildly after the tin plates.

Marguerite hastily scrambled to her feet, calling in alarm, "Gaston. Look at that enormous cloud. It is going to rain any minute now. Where is Vlas?"

"Still asleep. I'm afraid he is drunk."

"But what are we going to do if he can't drive?" Marguerite wailed. "I must get to Astrovo before nightfall, or they may send a messenger to grandmaman to tell her I never arrived."

"They won't have to. I can handle the horses as well as Vlas, but what to do about him?"

"I don't care if we leave him here. He had no business getting drunk. Let's start."

"Wait!" Gaston caught her by the ends of her sash. "I think he is coming to."

The coachman was on his feet. Swaying slightly, he approached the horses and began to fumble with the harness.

"Maybe he is not so drunk after all," Marguerite whispered.

Suddenly, Vlas took a step back, stared at the horses and

muttered, "Could swear we started with gray horses, and now look at them. Bay!" He wet his finger and gingerly rubbed the flank of the nearest horse. "Still bay," he announced, shaking his head.

"He *is* drunk," Gaston whispered. "He can't even remember the color of the horses he was driving. I think we should . . ."

Thunder drowned the rest of the sentence. Grabbing his sister around the waist, Gaston raced across the grass and pushed Marguerite into the coach just as a blue fork of lightning tore the black clouds. He ran back to gather up the picnic things.

The thunder seemed to sober Vlas. He snatched a blanket from under the coachman's seat, threw it over the horses' backs, and promptly dived under the coach himself. Another streak of lightning came. The animals rolled frightened eyes, straining at the harness.

"We should get away from these oaks. They're dangerous in a thunderstorm," Gaston commented, getting into the coach with the basket.

But it was impossible to get out. Rain was already falling in a solid sheet. Marguerite stared at the rain-streaked coach windows. "What are we going to do now? The roads will be impassable."

"The roads will be dry and dusty in no time," Gaston consoled her. "Look, it is not raining so hard now."

The worst of the storm was over. Strong gusts of wind were driving the clouds away, and it was only on the horizon that streaks of lightning still came and went.

Soon the sun came out, and the air was crisp and pure. Opening the window on his side, Gaston said, "Let's start, Vlas!"

The rutted road was negotiated somehow, with the coach leaning so far to one side that Marguerite's big hatbox slid across the floor. Once safely on the highway, Vlas straightened up, pulled his jacket tighter, and with a wild, "Oh, ho . . . ho . . . ho!" whipped the horses.

The coach sprang forward with a jolt that almost threw the two occupants off their seats. Gaston yelled out, "You fool! Where are you going? Astrovo is to the north!"

"North, south!" Vlas shouted, brandishing his whip. "Who cares! We go where our hearts go!" At these words he dropped one of the reins but managed to retrieve it before it got caught in the front wheels.

"Turn north!" Gaston ordered, leaning dangerously out of the window. "Immediately!"

His tone apparently had effect. Grumbling, the old coachman started to turn the coach.

"Gaston," Marguerite said anxiously, looking at the long shadows cast by the trees, "is it very late?"

"Let me see." He fished a big silver watch out of his pocket and snapped the lid open. "After six," he announced. "That *nalivka* of grandmaman's sent us all to sleep for almost two hours. Don't worry," he added hastily, as Marguerite's lips began to tremble. "The storm will make a good excuse for our being late. And grandmaman made arrangements for Vlas and myself to spend the night at Astrovo, so she can't possible find out anything about our little adventure. I only hope Vlas doesn't get us lost."

But they did get lost, several times. It was almost eight when the coach rolled into a long avenue of old elm trees. The sky was cloudy again and a slight drizzle was falling.

"Astrovo!" Vlas announced, pointing with his whip at the lighted windows at the end of the avenue.

"Marguerite, wake up! We have arrived." Gaston shook his sister, who was dozing in her corner.

"What did you say? Ah, yes, I see. Gaston, perhaps—"She stopped. "Why, how strange!"

"What is strange?"

"Hush!" Marguerite whispered. "Listen!"

"I can't hear anything. Wait." Gaston fumbled in the darkness and opened one of the windows. Bubbles of music floated into the coach.

"It's a gavotte!" Marguerite exclaimed. "They are giving a ball."

"A ball? I doubt it. Perhaps it is a dancing lesson."

"Not at this hour. Oh, here is the house. Tell Vlas to stop, quickly. We are getting out."

"What for? Well, if you want to . . ." Gaston gave the order to the coachman and followed Marguerite, who was already scrambling out.

They stood shoulder to shoulder, gazing at the house that loomed out of the darkness. It was curiously built. The central two-story part with a gabled roof towered above the two single-story wings. The right wing, long and slightly curving, was dark. The left wing, which was much shorter, showed three tall windows ablaze with lights.

"There is nothing," Marguerite murmured with disappointment.

Gaston turned to her. "What do you mean?"

"I thought I saw big flower beds and statues just like your friend had described, and I wanted to make sure, but look. . . ." Marguerite gestured toward the unkempt lawn visible in the light streaming from the windows. A circle of moss-grown stones in the center suggested that there might once have been a fountain.

"Not exactly the Garden of Eden," Gaston said. "Listen! There is the music again."

"Yes, and they are dancing." Marguerite watched the shadows flitter behind the high plate-glass windows. "Gaston! Something is wrong."

"What?"

"If the Astrovs were giving a ball, the whole house would be lit up, not just the ballroom."

"There are a few lights upstairs, and another one on the ground floor."

"But those are only bedroom candles and maybe an oil lamp. No, something is strange."

"Why don't we peep in? That's the best way to find out."

"Peep through those windows?" Marguerite shrank back. "We couldn't."

"Yes, we could. Come along." Gaston seized his sister's hand and they ran across the grass, past the marble steps leading to a wide terrace, and underneath the mysterious windows. "There is a ledge," he said quietly, groping among the jasmine bushes. "Let me lift you. That's right. Now grip the windowsill and hold tight."

In another moment, they were both peering into the gold-and-ivory ballroom.

"What a crowd!" Marguerite whispered. "But—it's a costume ball. Funny, they are not wearing masks. Look at those enormous side hoops and those feathers. . . . And the hairdos! See that lady turning her back to us? Her hair must be piled at least two feet high, and it is all hung with gold chains and flowers. I wonder how her head can hold it all."

"And the men!" Gaston whispered back. "Embroidered jackets, white silk breeches, silk stockings—wish I could dress like that!"

"They are dancing a minuet." Marguerite pressed her face closer against the windowpane. "It is almost over, I think. Now the footmen are coming with refreshments. That girl in the orange-and-silver gown resembles Ada. She seems nervous— look how she keeps opening and closing her fan."

Gaston answered something, but Marguerite was not listening. She was trying to guess who it could be that the orange-and-silver girl was watching so intently. Following her gaze, she saw a young couple standing not far from the window. A footman with a tray prevented Marguerite from seeing them better. She craned her neck but could only make out that the man was young and very tall, while his companion was a slender girl in blue brocade. She was obviously laughing at something he had said. Her shoulders were shaking and tendrils of chestnut hair, escaping the powdered coiffure, danced on the nape of her neck.

Marguerite glanced around for the girl in orange. She was now quite close to the couple, her face set, her dark eyes full of hate.

Forgetting the narrow ledge on which she balanced, Marguerite moved slightly to get a better view. Her foot slipped and she grasped her brother's arm for support. Caught unawares, he staggered, lost his balance, and fell into the bushes, taking Marguerite with him.

"Now what made you grab me like that?" he asked, annoyed. He scrambled up and helped Marguerite to her feet.

"I—I just slipped." Marguerite rubbed an aching elbow. "Please help me up again, Gaston, I want to—"

She broke off as they both raised their heads and gazed at the black windowpanes. . . .

4

Irina

Astrovo, May 17, 1818

Greatly honored and dearly beloved grandmaman:

I've been living here for exactly a week and your messenger is due tomorrow, so I must hasten and have this letter ready for him.

The next paragraph required careful handling. Marguerite laid down her quill and thought hard, a pucker between her brows. It would have been fun to describe the strange sight she and her brother had seen on the night of their arrival at Astrovo, but it was unthinkable. Such a story would only make her grandmother anxious and displeased.

Picking up her quill again, she wrote: *Gaston has probably told you that we were caught by a thunderstorm and arrived here somewhat late. The Astrovs were very understanding about it and served us a nice hot supper.*

Marguerite reread what she had written and smiled with sat-isfaction: *"somewhat late"* was truthful enough, though vague. She and Gaston had suddenly seen a light gleam under the front door and heard a woman's voice saying, "I am sure I heard a coach arrive, sister." They simply scuttled back to the coach and made Vlas drive them up to the house, pretending they had just arrived. Two elderly ladies were on the threshold waiting for them. Entering the house, Marguerite had almost expected to see the hall full of guests saying good-bye, but instead there was only an old manservant, bowing and mutter-ing greetings. The big chandelier was unlit; a solitary candle burned in a sconce, dimly lighting the oak-paneled walls. It had been strange and rather frightening. After a good night's rest, though, the incident of the ball seemed a dream and after a week of her new life, it became a hazy memory.

Marguerite's thoughts went back to her letter. *There are four girls here besides myself,* she wrote. *Two of them are twins, Pachette and Annette Liubimov. They look alike, both very fair and pink-cheeked. When they don't talk it is hard to tell them apart, but once they start it is easy because Pachette talks all the time, while Annette only repeats her sister's last words. They live not too far from Astrovo and their mother keeps sending them big baskets of food, mostly cakes and sweets. The twins stuff themselves all day long, which is why they are so plump.*

Lily Markova lives almost a hundred miles away. She was sent to Astrovo because she does not get along with her stepmother. Her father married again about a year ago and Lily simply hates his new wife, even though she does not remember her own mother. She has bright red hair and would be quite pretty if she were not constantly pouting. Yesterday she got a letter from home and tore it up without opening it. Then she cried for hours and tried to put the pieces together, but couldn't.

There is nothing much to say about Myra Korsak. She is sixteen, but looks older because she is so tall and thin, and her shoulders are rounded a little, I suppose from too much studying. I tried to be friendly with her, but she does not talk much. Another pupil is supposed to arrive any day. That will make six of us.

I have a large room all to myself. It is called "the blue room" but everything is so faded and threadbare, it is hard to tell the color. The bed is comfortable, but the canopy sags a bit. There are holes in the rug, but the furniture is arranged in such a way that they don't show.

I am really quite happy here, grandmaman, and you were right, it is fun to be with other girls of my own age. Mademoiselle Ada is a very good teacher, though rather cold. Mademoiselle Vanda is a dear. She showed me a new stitch. I won't bother you with it, I know how you hate needlework. I am a bit afraid of Mademoiselle Malvina. Monsieur Erast is nice—he teaches botany—but I think he is afraid of us girls. Monsieur Nicolas teaches history and seems surprised when one of us asks an intelligent question!

You are probably going to wonder why I use all these first names. There is a good reason for this. The late Papa Astrov was called Anufrii. Can you imagine calling anyone Malvina Anu . . . fri . . . yev . . . na? I can't even spell it! There is also a plain Mademoiselle here, who used to be governess to Mademoiselle Malvina and her sister. When one of us pupils asks her anything, she waves her hands and screams, "Comprends pas! Comprends pas!"

We girls are addressed by our first names because it is supposed to make us feel more at home. Not by men of course; it wouldn't be polite.

There are not many servants. Lavrentii, the footman, is very old and just potters around, duster in hand. The cook is old too, but no one ever sees her. Besides the cook, there are two maids. Outside the house, there are a couple of grooms at the stable, a coachman, and an old gardener who is supposed to look after the grounds, but doesn't. Of course that is not enough staff for an estate like Astrovo. Mademoiselle Malvina told us quite firmly that we are supposed to dress and undress without help. I *don't mind, but Lily makes such a fuss every morning because there is no one to help her do her hair. Which reminds me . . .*

Marguerite stared at the paper, wondering whether she should tell her grandmother something that had been bothering her and that she could not explain. Why not? she thought, and bent over her writing desk again.

Two days ago, I was awakened very early by a voice that sounded like a parrot's, screaming, "She is ugly. Ugly! Ugly!" It frightened me because it sounded so vicious, as if the parrot hated the person who was ugly. I got out of bed and opened my door, but everything was quiet. The strange part is that later, when I mentioned this to Mademoiselle Malvina, she looked annoyed and told me there was no parrot in the house, and that I must have dreamed it. I know I did not and—

A rumble of wheels made Marguerite drop her quill and rush to the window.

In another moment, she was back at her desk. *I am going to finish this letter a little later, grandmaman. Someone has just arrived. I think it is the new girl.*

In a flash of white muslin skirts, Marguerite ran out of her room, along the corridor, and onto the landing. Leaning over the banisters, she saw Lavrentii usher two visitors into the hall.

One, a stout, middle-aged woman, was wrapped in a dark-red Turkish shawl with a long fringe that reached her knees. One hand clutched a lacy parasol while the other kept a grip on her hat, laden with ribbons and feathers.

Her companion was about Marguerite's age or maybe a little older. She was stuffed into a yellow silk gown that clashed with the pink ribbons of her bonnet. When the girl turned her head, Marguerite saw two deep blue eyes under dark, arched eyebrows. Clusters of blond curls with tinges of gold escaped from under the bonnet.

Curious, Marguerite leaned farther over the banisters, but

the sound of footsteps made her spring back. Malvina entered the hall, and Lavrentii promptly disappeared.

At the sight of Malvina, the woman bowed from the waist. "We're the Makarovs," she announced, straightening up again. The girl just stared.

Malvina looked startled for a moment, then returned the bow with a curt nod. "Yes, we were expecting you. So this is your daughter." She turned to the girl, who stood with her arms hanging, her mouth slightly open.

Her mother gave her a poke. "Greet the lady, Irina."

The girl started to bow, but Malvina stopped her with a quick gesture. "*Here* we curtsy," she said drily. "This will be one of the subjects of your deportment classes."

The mother and daughter both blinked.

"It means learning how to behave in society," Malvina explained in an icy tone. She went on, softening her voice somewhat, "Will you please step into my study so that we can attend to . . . er . . . business."

"Oh, we've got the money," the woman assured her, stuffing the umbrella under her arm and snatching at the big reticule hanging from her wrist.

As the group was crossing the hall, the woman said, "Five hundred rubles is a great deal of money! But then her father wants to make a lady of her. And the house! He had it refurbished from top to bottom. Gilded furniture! Now what do we need gilded furniture for? I asked him, and . . ."

The hall door closed and Marguerite did not catch the rest. For a moment she stood by the banisters, thinking. The proper thing to do would be to go back to her room and finish the letter to her grandmother. But the new girl interested her too much. Running down the stairway, she crossed the hall and entered the big drawing room into which Malvina's study opened. From behind the closed door came muffled voices. The five hundred rubles were probably being paid.

One could not just stand and stare at the door. Marguerite went to a small table between two windows and began to rearrange sprays of lilac in a crystal vase.

"Ah, Marguerite! I am glad you happen to be here, my dear." Marguerite turned and saw Malvina coming out of her study, the new girl at her heels.

"This is Mademoiselle Irina Makarova," Malvina told Marguerite. "But we will call you simply Irina." She laid her hand on the girl's shoulder. "Irina, this is Marguerite de Gramont, one of your companions."

Marguerite curtsied. Irina attempted to curtsy too, caught at the door jamb, and announced cheerfully, "My feet got hooked around each other."

Malvina winced. "Will you kindly take Irina to the mauve room, Marguerite. You know which one it is, don't you? Ada is giving a singing lesson to Lily." She went into the study and closed the door behind her.

After a moment of awkward silence, Irina said in the same cheerful voice, "I recognized you right away. Saw you in church with your grandmother this Easter."

Marguerite smiled. "It is nice of you to remember me. I may have seen you too.

"You wouldn't have," Irina said bluntly. "I wouldn't be in front with the gentry."

Marguerite felt embarrassed. "Shall we go upstairs now?" she asked. "The pupils sleep on the second floor, and so does Mademoiselle Ada. The rest of the family have their bedrooms downstairs, in the right wing."

"That Mamzelle Ada is her niece, isn't she?" Irina asked, pointing at the study door.

Marguerite murmured, "Yes."

When the girls reached Irina's room they found her trunk standing in the middle of the floor.

"You may want to change into something lighter," Marguerite suggested, looking at the heavy silk of Irina's gown.

"It certainly makes me itch," Irina agreed, "and that thing gives me a headache." She took her bonnet off and threw it on the bed. A sunbeam touched her head, and the blond tresses gleamed with deep gold.

"You have beautiful hair," Marguerite said sincerely.

Irina's lips trembled. "It *used* to be beautiful. I had a braid down to my knees, thick like a fist. It went three times around my head. Then Papasha got all that money. 'You make her fashionable,' he told Mamasha. So she calls a barber. He cuts my hair short, then rolls what is left into these sausages." She pulled at a limp curl as if trying to tear it out by the roots.

Marguerite agreed that a crown of braids must have suited Irina much better than those badly done curls, but she said gently, "Your hair has not been properly curled. If you will let me, I will put it up in *papillotes* tonight—I mean, in little strips of cloth. You will see how nice it is after it is combed out."

Irina gave her a broad smile. "Thank you. Now I suppose I had better change."

Opening the trunk, she took out a violently blue silk dress with an enormous flounce at the bottom. "Will this do?" she asked. Marguerite suppressed a shudder and shook her head.

After Irina had produced four more silk gowns, Marguerite asked, "Didn't you bring any light dresses? We all wear dimity, or lawn, or muslin, usually white."

"Papasha gave orders to have me rigged out in silks," Irina said. "A dressmaker stayed in our house for weeks, making these. But I have white things too." She dug deeper into the trunk and extracted a white muslin, its skirt loaded with blue bows.

"This will do," Marguerite said. "We can unpack the rest of your things later. When you are ready, I shall take you to the library. We are supposed to have a German lesson at eleven."

Walking along the corridor, the two girls came face to face with Mademoiselle. The old lady pulled her faded green shawl tightly around her and screamed, *"Comprends pas!"*

Irina's eyes became round. "Who is that madwoman?" she asked in a low voice.

Marguerite explained and added, "She is supposed to pretend she does not understand Russian so that we have to speak French to her."

Irina laughed. "Well, if she speaks to me in French, it is *I* who will scream that I don't understand, and no pretense about it." She suddenly stopped laughing as they approached the library. Marguerite felt a little nervous too, wondering how Irina was going to be received.

But everything went smoothly. Ada came forward, demure in her gray gown. She greeted Irina and introduced the other pupils.

Irina did not try to bow. Apparently mindful of Malvina's words, she made a plunge that only vaguely resembled a curtsy, and sat down at the table between Annette and Pachette. Myra pushed toward the newcomer a sheet of paper and a quill. "For you to take notes," she murmured shyly.

Lily bent over the table and said, "Did Marguerite tell you why I am here? It is because my stepmother hates me."

These confidences were interrupted by Ada. Opening a book, she announced, "I shall now read a sentence in German and you will all please write it down." Turning to Irina, she asked, "Do you know any German?"

"Some. Papasha buys fruit and vegetables from two Germans who have a garden near Tula. I often listen to them talking when they deliver the goods. *Guten morgen . . . guten tag . . . ein, zwei, drei . . . verflucht . . .*"

At the last word, the twins began to shake with laughter. Marguerite gasped.

Ada said, "We do not use swear words here. Kindly remember it for the future."

"Swear word? I didn't know it was." Irina seemed sincerely surprised. "Those Germans always use it when Papasha tries to underpay them. But that is trade."

"I am afraid none of us knows much about trade," Ada answered shortly. "And now, let us begin. Here is the first sentence. . . ."

After the German lesson came lunch. Marguerite watched with horror as Irina held the knife in her fist and bent low over her plate.

Nicolas and Erast observed the newcomer—Erast furtively and with shocked surprise, Nicolas openly and with amusement.

Having finished her meat, Irina picked up a slice of bread and began to mop her plate with it.

"More bread, mademoiselle?" Nicolas inquired, offering her the breadbasket.

Irina shook her head. "No, thank you. I am full." She patted her middle and hiccuped.

"Just a spoonful of gravy then?" Nicolas insisted gallantly.

"I couldn't, thank you."

Vanda swayed with dismay, while Malvina said with restrained fury, "*Please,* Nicolas."

Marguerite was not surprised when after lunch Malvina said to Irina, "Please stay, my dear. I want to have a talk with you."

It seemed unkind to abandon her charge now, so Marguerite waited anxiously by the dining-room door.

"Was she very severe with you?" she asked, when the victim finally emerged.

Irina answered indifferently, "Oh, no. She just talked and talked. You hold your spoon like this and your knife like that. If I did all she wants me to do, I would never have time for a bit of food. Where are we going now?"

"After lunch, we usually go to our rooms to study or to write letters," Marguerite explained. "Later this afternoon, Monsieur Erast is going to take us all for a long walk. It is called a botany lesson. He will talk about how ferns grow and what they are called in Latin."

Irina yawned widely. "Talk again! That is all they do in this house."

5

The Blooming Fern

A little before three, all the pupils assembled on the terrace. Mademoiselle Vanda, who was to be their chaperon, appeared, almost hidden under a parasol of yellowed lace. She told the girls that Ada was not going to join them. She had a bad headache and was lying down.

"Have you not brought a parasol?" Marguerite asked Irina, opening her own pink one.

"Don't need it. Why hide from God's sun?" Irina looked at the radiantly blue sky.

"I have not brought a parasol either," Myra declared, joining them. "I must have both hands free to take notes."

Marguerite enjoyed the walks, but it had never occurred to her to write down Erast's comments on the insides of a flower, or his explanation as to how the bark grows on trees.

Myra touched her arm. "Mademoiselle Vanda is calling us. Let's go."

The group of girls, their white frocks bright against the

greenery, followed Erast's tall, stooping figure, while Vanda trailed behind them. They passed through what remained of the flower garden and turned into the narrow avenue leading through the park. Gray moss grew between the roots of giant old trees, whose branches made a dense dome over the girls' heads.

"Brr. . . ." Annette shivered. "It is more a forest than a park. I am always afraid there might be wild animals here."

"There are," Lily assured her with an unkind smile. "In winter one can hear wolves howl."

They were leaving the park, and the avenue they followed forked around an old stone urn. To the right it widened into a dirt road, while to the left it became a mere path.

Erast, glancing nervously at the girls behind him, turned left toward a small birch grove.

"Where does that other road go?" Irina asked, glancing over her shoulder.

"To the village and past the apiary," Marguerite explained. Noticing Irina's blank stare, she added, "That is where Monsieur Erast keeps his bees."

"One beehive is made of glass," Myra remarked. "One can watch the bees at work."

"We have not been invited to the apiary so far." Marguerite laughed. "Just as well. I am afraid of bees."

"Just a few more minutes, mesdemoiselles," Erast assured them as they entered the birch grove. "Here! Straight on." They followed him down a winding path. The ground sloped suddenly and a small creek came in sight. The girls cautiously approached the edge and peered down at a shallow brook trickling between luxuriant clumps of ferns.

Erast rubbed his thin hands. "May I have your attention, please, mesdemoiselles."

Vanda settled herself on a nearby boulder, tucking stray

wisps of graying hair under her bonnet. Marguerite sat down beside her and pretended to shake a pebble out of her shoe. Immediately, two watery-blue eyes gazed at her. "I remember so well those days I walked here with my fiancé," Vanda said in a trembling voice. "One day, he carved our initials on a tree trunk. I remember too . . ."

This was worse than learning about ferns. Marguerite murmured something and joined the other girls, hoping that Erast had not noticed her absence.

To her relief, Lily distracted his attention. "At home, we had a beautiful big fern growing in front of the house. But my stepmother had it moved to the back of the garden and had a silly rosebush planted instead. Wasn't it hateful of her?"

Erast coughed. "Perhaps it was just as well. Roses like being in the sun, but ferns prefer shady places."

Myra was peering shortsightedly at her notebook. "I hope I got the Latin name right," she murmured.

"Does it matter?" Marguerite asked indifferently.

Myra looked hurt. "Of course it does. I must learn every bit of what they teach us here. My family is not rich and I have two little sisters. I am going to teach them."

The lesson over, everybody started back home. The sun was still high in the sky, the meadows studded with spring flowers. A swallow flew so low, it almost touched Marguerite's shoulder.

Pachette, who was carrying a small spray of fern, touched it with her finger. "It looks like a green feather," she remarked. "What a pity it does not flower, it would be even prettier."

"A pity," her sister echoed.

Irina, who had been silent throughout the lesson, suddenly regained her speech. "Of course it flowers!"

Erast, walking behind the girls, said with a smile, "I am

afraid you are mistaken, Mademoiselle Irina. Ferns do not bloom."

"They do though!" Irina turned around and faced him. "Every year, on June the twenty-fourth, the eve of Ivan Kupala, at midnight, the ferns bloom. Just one big red flower, like this." She cupped her hands to show the size of the flower. "It glows like flame and anyone who picks it can find a buried treasure. The flower gives him that power."

"Hidden treasure!" Myra exclaimed eagerly. "Where?"

Irina shrugged. "Oh, anywhere. People often hid gold coins or jewelry in olden times."

"Allow me, please." Erast raised his hand. "It is quite true that people used to bury their valuables when an enemy invasion was expected. Even in our times, when Napoleon—" He broke off, his face suddenly pale, and stared at something over Irina's shoulder.

Lily seized Marguerite's hand and whispered, "Look!"

They were just a few feet away from the stone urn. From the direction of the apiary, a middle-aged woman in a dark dress with a white shawl crisscrossed at the waist was running, stumbling, and running again. She was gesturing wildly and screaming something that Marguerite could not catch.

Lily exclaimed, "Who is she? What's happened?" Erast stood motionless, his eyes glazed.

Vague Mademoiselle Vanda suddenly took charge of the situation. Her face set, her mittened hand clutching the handle of her parasol so tightly that Marguerite was sure it would break, she ordered the girls to move on. "It is only a poor woman from the village who is out of her mind," she told them. "The kindest thing to do is to ignore her."

"But," Pachette protested, "she seems to be calling for help. Couldn't we—"

Vanda cut her short. "She doesn't need any help. I have explained to you already that she is out of her mind."

The girls walked on, whispering among themselves. As they passed the stone urn, Marguerite looked back. The woman had disappeared. Where could she have gone? Marguerite wondered. The road was quite straight and one could see for a good distance.

She asked herself the same question that evening after supper, while sitting in the drawing room and waiting for Nicolas's history lesson.

Nicolas objected to the pupils sitting around the library table on straight-backed chairs. "I like to be comfortable, and I want other people to be comfortable too," he had declared. So the girls were grouped all over the vast drawing room. The twins were playing ticktacktoe at a small table. Lily had drawn Irina over to a love seat by the window and was whispering something into her ear. In the corner opposite, Myra was knitting diligently at something long and gray that looked like a child's camisole.

Marguerite moved closer to her. "I can't help thinking about that peasant woman. . . ." she began.

Without raising her eyes, Myra answered quietly, "She was not a peasant."

"Not a peasant? But Mademoiselle Vanda said . . ."

"Yes," Myra said thoughtfully. "For some reason, Mademoiselle Vanda wanted us to believe it was a woman from the village. But she was not dressed like one. Did you see that little white cap on her head? And the bunch of keys at her belt? She looked like a housekeeper to me."

"But why would a housekeeper run on the road screaming?"

Myra gave her a serious look. "Did you actually *hear* her scream?"

"Nn . . . o, not really," Marguerite admitted. "But her mouth was open and—and I *thought* I heard her scream."

Myra nodded. "I did too. We all did. But thinking back, I realize I didn't hear a sound."

"The woman was quite far away."

Myra frowned. "That is another strange thing. She was distant, yes, but she was also running hard, and yet she never seemed to come closer. Oh, here is Mademoiselle Ada!"

The drawing-room door opened and Ada came in. Her face looked pale and her black hair was damp in front and gave off a faint smell of vinegar. "Yes, my headache is much better, thank you," she replied to the girls' inquiries and stepped back for her uncle Nicolas.

The pupils rose and curtsied. Nicolas's bad leg was evidently better for instead of his usual growl he smiled and bowed. The smile reminded Marguerite of the statue of a satyr she had once seen in a park.

Lowering himself into an armchair, Nicolas addressed the girls. "Last time, mesdemoiselles, we talked about Peter the Great and his reforms. This evening we will talk about St. Petersburg, the capital of Russia, which he founded." With another smile, he turned to Irina. "I understand from my niece Ada that you have displayed an extraordinary knowledge of German, mademoiselle, and my brother was astonished by your information on botany. Perhaps you would care to tell us what you know about the foundation of St. Petersburg?"

Irina answered readily. "I do know something about it. The sexton of our parish church often talked about Peter the Great. He had a picture of him, too. In *color*. Bought it at a fair. Handsome man he was—Peter the Great, I mean."

"I see. Most interesting." Nicolas rubbed his hands in anticipation. "If you please, mademoiselle, step in front of the class and tell us what the sexton said about Peter the Great and St. Petersburg."

"Yes, I can do that." Irina got up and faced the other pupils. Ada's pale face flushed and she threw an angry glance in her uncle's direction. Vanda, who had just slipped in and sat down with a piece of embroidery in her hand, looked anxious.

"Once Peter the Great took a walk along the shore of the Neva," Irina began. "There was nothing around, no trees, no grass, only marshes and marshes, miles of them. But he said, 'I want a town to stand here!' and ordered thousands and thousands of workmen to start digging. So they dug and dug, and built dams and foundations for houses. But soon the marsh fevers got them and they died. Then more workmen came, and went on digging and building. They, too, died, and so it went until the town was ready. But even now"—Irina's deep voice became huskier—"the souls of those dead workmen roam around St. Petersburg every night. They all curse the emperor and scream, 'Malediction! Malediction!' "

She was interrupted by a hysterical scream. "Don't! Don't say that! Do you hear me?" Ada sprang from her seat and took a threatening step in Irina's direction.

"What is the meaning of this scene? Nicolas! I thought you were giving these young ladies a history lesson." Malvina stood in the doorway, her gaze going from Ada to her brother.

Rushing across the room, Ada hid her face on Vanda's shoulder. "Make her stop! Please, make her stop."

"Yes, my dear, yes. Come with me." Vanda led her niece out of the room.

"Kindly attend to your lesson, mesdemoiselles." Malvina followed them.

Nicolas muttered something under his breath, and began to talk rapidly about the law that Peter the Great had made prohibiting men to wear beards.

As soon as the lesson was over, Lavrentii shuffled in with a tray of hot chocolate and cookies, the usual sign for the girls to retire to their bedrooms.

The big oil lamp in the drawing room and the candelabras in the library were extinguished, but in the bedrooms candles burned on for a long time.

Sitting at her writing desk, Myra toiled over a letter to her mother. *I was grieved to receive the sad news, about the little ones having measles and Papa losing his lawsuit. I only wish I could help—* Myra dabbed at her eyes with a crumpled handkerchief and went on. *I know that Papa had to borrow some money to send me to Astrovo and I am doing my best to learn whatever they teach us here. Today we had a botany lesson. . . .*

From the twins' room came low voices. Curled up at the foot of Annette's bed, Pachette was saying earnestly, "I assure you I did not dream it. It happened last Monday. No, Tuesday. I was standing on the terrace, watching the sunset, and I saw a group of men in old-fashioned clothes coming up the avenue to the house. They seemed to be carrying something heavy between them."

"Couldn't you see what it was?" Annette asked.

"No, they were too far away. But I did see a woman walking alongside them and wringing her hands, and"—Pachette's voice sank with every word—"she was the same woman we saw on the road this afternoon."

"Oh." Annette paused. "Then what?"

"Nothing. The sun was in my eyes. I blinked and when I looked again there was no one in the avenue."

"Oo . . . oo, I am frightened." Annette gulped, snuggling deeper into the bed. "Do you think we ought to write to Papa and ask him to take us home?"

"Certainly not. Remember what he said. We can't make our debut until we learn more French and dancing and other things. We must stay on. But there are strange things going on here; I wish we could find out more about them."

At the other end of the house, Nicolas was expressing the same opinion, though in somewhat different words. "So *they* are on the rampage again," he grumbled, untying his neck scarf in front of a mirror. "Perhaps we should invite them all to dinner and find out just what they are after."

Lavrentii, who was bringing in a jug of hot water, paled. "Heaven be with us. Don't you talk like that," he muttered, crossing himself.

"Just a friendly chat over a goblet of wine," Nicolas teased.

Lavrentii was not listening. Repeating, "Heaven be with us," he began to pour hot water into the washbasin, spilling most of it on the floor.

Vanda's room smelled of the camomile tisane that Mademoiselle had prepared on a spirit lamp. The tisane was too sweet; Mademoiselle, who did not see well, had put in too much sugar. But Vanda, sitting up in bed, drank it gratefully. It did not matter. At least Mademoiselle was company. "I couldn't bear being alone. I just couldn't," Vanda murmured to herself, wrapping her woolen shawl snugly around her shoulders.

Malvina, on the contrary, enjoyed the solitude of her room. Bent over the household books, she added long columns of figures, anxiously comparing the *In* and *Out* totals. The pupils' money helped, of course. Some of the mortgage had been paid off, and the long-overdue bill for horse feed was settled at last. Still, expenses had to be cut down. The girls' hot chocolate, for instance, could be made with water instead of milk, or— A knock on the door made Malvina raise her head. Erast slipped in. "Sorry I disturbed you, sister. May I speak with you?"

"About what?" Malvina looked at her half brother's brown frock coat. It was worn out, almost threadbare in some places. Another expense coming up. "Do say what you have to say, Erast, and let me get back to my accounts."

He cleared his throat. "Well, you must have heard from Vanda what happened this afternoon."

"I did. It is not important."

"Oh, but it is!" Coming closer to the table, Erast whispered, "Malvina, please listen to me, just this once. Something is wrong again. For a while it was quiet, but now. . . . The servants are talking and I—I have forebodings. You know what happened before."

"Almost sixty years ago."

Erast smiled sadly. "I may be a fool, Malvina. Perhaps there are no grounds for my fears, but I still think we should not have these girls here. Why not send them home?"

"And return the money to their parents?"

"Naturally."

"No!" Malvina stood up, her giant shadow swerving across the wall. "That money is for Astrovo. I am going to save our family estate, at all costs."

Erast went out, closing the door softly behind him.

Three bedrooms were dark. From Irina's bed came deep, peaceful breathing. Marguerite, on the contrary, slept fitfully, haunted by nightmares. One was especially vivid. Gaston was drowning in a foamy, raging river while she ran along the shore holding out her hands to him. But she could not reach him, and he was carried farther and farther away by the waves.

Lily was in bed, too, but not asleep. There was a communicating door between her bedroom and that of the twins. It was locked and masked by a dressing table, but Lily could hear what was said on the other side and listened avidly to Pachette's story about the strange people in the avenue.

"She is making it all up, and I am not afraid," Lily kept telling herself, wishing she dared to reach out her hand and light her bedside candle. Suddenly she longed to be back at home with her stepmother.

6

Gaston

Nightmares continued to plague Marguerite all through the week. One night was especially exhausting and it was only toward morning that she finally dozed off.

The sound of horses' hoofs underneath her window woke her. Who could be coming so early? she wondered, turning her pillow over and settling down more comfortably.

But she had no time to go to sleep again. There was a knock at her door and the squeaky voice of Liubasha, the younger of the two maids, announced, "Miss, your brother has just arrived."

"Gaston!" Marguerite leaped out of bed and, throwing on a blue robe, opened the door. "My brother? Where is he?"

"In the hall, miss. He arrived on horseback just now. Mademoiselle Malvina is with him."

"I am coming." Marguerite raced along the corridor. Her

blue bedroom slippers kept falling off, so she kicked them off and carried them as she hurried down the stairway.

When she looked over the banisters, she saw her brother's face gray with fatigue. She flew down the few remaining steps and threw herself into his arms. "Gaston, something is very wrong. I can see it from the way you look. Is it grandmaman? Is she sick? Tell me!"

He smiled. "Now, little sister, calm yourself. Grandmaman is in good health. But two maids were taken ill during the night. As soon as grandmaman realized it was smallpox, she packed me off immediately with a letter to mademoiselle, asking her to shelter me for a few weeks while the house is in quarantine."

"You are going to live here!" Marguerite exclaimed. "How wonderful!"

At the sound of Marguerite's voice, Malvina looked up from the letter. "We are of course delighted to offer you our hospitality, Count," she said. "Yes, delighted." Her gaze shifted to Marguerite's bare feet and stayed there.

Gaston looked embarrassed. "Please, mademoiselle, I am hardly ever addressed as Count."

Malvina smiled, "Very well. We will simply call you Monsieur Gaston then, since you are Marguerite's brother. Your room will be ready in a little while. In the meantime, perhaps you would care to take a walk in the grounds. We breakfast at eight."

"Certainly, mademoiselle. I will see you at breakfast, sister." He vanished through the door leading to the terrace.

Marguerite put on her slippers and ran up the stairway. She found her room flooded with sunshine. Usually, when she woke up the sun was already high over the treetops. She watched the crystal bottles on her dressing table sparkle and shimmer. Although the sunlight was pleasant, it made the furniture and hangings look even shabbier. Now with so much light, she could see something round and dark in the middle of the canopy, where it sagged worst.

Curious, Marguerite took her parasol and poked at the canopy. The dark object bounced out and fell onto the floor. She picked it up gingerly. It was a ball made of red and yellow silk and filled with something that felt like sawdust. She flicked off a thick layer of dust, and the silk glowed.

For several minutes, Marguerite stood staring at the ball in her hand, trying to imagine how it came to be on top of the canopy. A child must have thrown it. Was it Ada's? It could be. . . .

Marguerite put the ball on top of her writing desk and began to dress. Anxious to make her brother proud, she spent so much time getting ready that she started when her little china clock chimed eight. At the same time there was a soft plonk behind her. She turned around to see the silken ball roll off the desk and onto the floor. That was strange; it had been securely wedged between a candlestick and a book. As Marguerite bent down to retrieve the ball, she felt someone brush against her. There came the scent of a perfume that smelled like roses, and yet not roses.

I am imagining things, Marguerite told herself, placing the ball back on the desk. She gave a last glance at her mirror and ran out of the room, the long ends of her sash streaming behind her.

The pupils were already gathered in the dining room. Ada was talking French with Mademoiselle and trying to get the other girls to take part in the conversation.

Vanda was apparently still asleep. She always came to breakfast late. The men were never present. Erast went to his apiary at dawn, and Nicolas was served by Lavrentii in his room.

Malvina stood by the window and impatiently tapped the glass with her finger. At Marguerite's entrance she turned around. "I am afraid your brother has lost his way in the park. However, we will wait for him a few more minutes." She consulted the small golden watch hanging on a chain around her neck. "By the way, have you seen Irina? She must be still asleep and— Oh!" She stared as Irina appeared in the doorway, Gaston at her heels.

Her face pink, and stains of wet grass on her white skirt, Irina cried cheerfully, "Good morning! I got up with the sun. It was beautiful. Birds were singing and there was dew everywhere. I washed my face with it. Good for the skin! Then I met her brother."

Gaston muttered, "Mademoiselle was kind enough to show me the stables."

"We fed the horses. I had some bread with me, and we got salt from the groom."

Malvina ignored her. "I will now introduce you to these young ladies," she told Gaston, "and then we will proceed with breakfast. It is late."

The exchange of bows and curtsies was brief. Gaston seated himself beside his sister and breakfast began. The ladylike conversation around the table was interrupted by Irina. "I am so hungry, I could eat an ox!"

Ada looked at her. "Is your cup so heavy, you have to hold it in both hands?" she asked. Her tone was light, but there was a tinge of venom in it.

Irina answered indifferently, "My hands are cold." She took a long sip of her tea. "Ah, it is good to have something hot after the morning chill. You should see Papasha drink tea. Ten glasses are nothing to him."

"My cup is chipped on one side. It is most unpleasant," Lily complained.

"But Papasha would never touch tea after being drunk," Irina continued, her deep voice drowning out Lily's. "He would only take pickle water."

"What is it?" Mademoiselle asked. "What would he drink?"

"That will do, Irina." Turning to Gaston, Malvina asked, "How did you like the park?"

Seeing her brother at a loss to find a suitable compliment, Marguerite came to his rescue. "We have no park at home," she said. "I always enjoy walking under those big trees."

Malvina smiled approvingly and remarked that Pachette's pink dress suited her complexion.

The gracious atmosphere was barely reestablished when Irina broke it again. Leaning across Marguerite, she peered into Gaston's cup. "Oh! Oh! You are going on a long voyage. See how the tea leaves are stretched out."

"Where? Where? Let me see!" the twins cried in one voice, craning their necks. "Do you know how to tell fortunes with tea leaves?"

"Of course I can read the tea leaves," Irina answered. "I learned it from an old fortune-teller who lives in Tula behind the fish market. Mamasha and me often go to see her."

"Do look at mine. I can see something like a circle." Pachette pushed her teacup across the table. Her sister immediately did the same. The cups collided with a crash, spilling tea on the tablecloth.

"My Sèvres china!" Malvina's scream came from the heart.

Before she had time to say anything else, Ada intervened. Standing up, her dark eyes flashing, she turned on Irina. "Those two have behaved like children, but it is you who caused it all. And there is nothing to laugh about," she added, looking at Lily, who was gloating.

What a fuss! Marguerite thought, watching Ada's angry expression. For two broken cups . . . She could be forty instead of eighteen. No one spoke much during the rest of breakfast, and the girls seemed only too glad to escape from the dining room.

Later in the morning, Marguerite went to the drawing room to practice on the piano. She was getting out her music when she heard Gaston's voice under the window. Another voice answered. Ada's? Marguerite tiptoed to the window and looked out.

Her brother was pretending to hide behind an old oak with a circular bench around the trunk. "No, no, I dare not come out before I see you smile, Mademoiselle Ada. You frightened me too much at breakfast today. I am still shaking."

"I am in charge of these young ladies." Ada's lips were curving.

She looks so much prettier in that white frock than in her usual gray one, Marguerite thought. Ah! She is smiling. No one can resist Gaston.

"Thank you for a most charming smile." Gaston emerged from behind the tree. "But what is this?" He picked up from the bench a light wooden hoop and two slender wooden sticks with handles. "A *cerceau!* Would you favor me with a game, Mademoiselle Ada? Please!"

"I haven't played since school." Ada took the stick and poised herself.

The hoop flew through the air. She deftly caught it on her stick and with a flick of her wrist sent it back in Gaston's direction. Under the admiring eyes of Marguerite, the hoop flew from one player to the other. At last Ada missed. "Forfeit! Forfeit!" Gaston called out. "Now what is it going to be? I know! You must let me look at your palm and tell you your fortune."

Ada's ringing laugh surprised Marguerite so much, she almost lost her balance. Clutching at the window frame, she saw Ada hold out her hand and Gaston bend over her.

Suddenly, Ada drew back. From around the corner of the house, Irina appeared. "I looked out and saw you playing with those things," she called, waving her hand. "I want to play, too."

"Certainly. I was just going inside. It is time for Lily's music lesson." Ada threw her stick on the bench and walked away.

Marguerite returned to the piano, feeling somehow let down. She wondered vaguely if Ada felt the same.

That afternoon, Malvina announced that they were going to have a musical evening.

"Am I expected to perform too?" Gaston whispered to his sister as they were taking their seats in the drawing room.

Marguerite laughed. "You are supposed to listen and applaud our talents."

The performance was opened by Vanda, singing an old French ballad about a girl who refused to give a rose to her lover. At the last lines,

> *"I wish that the rose were still on the bush,*
> *And that my friend Pierre still loved me. . . ."*

she bent her head low over the keys and began to sob softly. No one paid any attention.

Marguerite nudged her brother. "Ada is going to sing now," she whispered. "Do compliment her afterward. She will be pleased."

"Even if I don't like her singing?"

"Even then. I think," Marguerite added, "Ada is a little sweet on you."

"Sweet on me! What a calamity! Say, I have an idea . . . I am going to court your friend, what is her name . . . Irina. So your respected preceptress will realize that my heart is already taken."

Marguerite giggled. "Hush! Mademoiselle Malvina is speaking."

"Ada, my dear," Malvina said, "will you sing that aria from—"

She was interrupted by Nicolas, who had chosen to honor the gathering with his presence. With a smile that again reminded Marguerite of a satyr, he asked Irina, "Would you enchant us with a song, mademoiselle?"

She beamed at him. "I could, but I only know simple songs, not about roses and things."

"A simple song then," Nicolas insisted, ignoring his half sister's glances.

Gaston immediately sprang to his feet. "Mademoiselle Irina, may I turn the pages for you?"

Irina stared at him. "What pages? The music, you mean? I wouldn't know how to read those crooks."

Malvina said icily, "Someone will have to accompany you, since you don't play the piano."

"Eh, who needs tinkle, tinkle?" Irina rose and, holding the back of a chair, began to sing.

> *"In the woods above the river*
> *Sometimes one can hear*
> *Cuckoo, cuckoo, cucko . . . o . . . oo."*

The rich, deep voice soared effortlessly, filled the vast drawing room, and made Nicolas raise his gray eyebrows in surprise.

Gaston leaned forward, whispering to Marguerite, "Why, she is superb!"

When the last *cuckoo* of the refrain had died away, Nicolas cried, "Bravo!" and the girls broke into excited chatter.

Vanda asked, "My dear, who taught you to sing like this?"

Irina shrugged. "Nobody. I just sing."

Nicolas nodded. "Assuredly. With such a voice, you just sing."

Malvina said briefly, "Very nice," and turned to her niece. "Now, Ada . . ."

"I could never sing after such a magnificent performance," Ada answered with such coldness that her aunt did not dare to insist.

The rest of the musical evening was not a success. Lily played the harp after warning the audience that she had not as yet quite mastered the instrument. "Then why play at all," Nicolas grumbled after she had finished.

The twins tried to sing a duet but broke into giggles and had to give up in the middle. Myra recited a poem in a singsong voice.

Marguerite pleaded a headache. It was not an excuse. Several restless nights, the early rising, and the excitement of Gaston's arrival had proved too much for her. I feel so tired, she thought, having said good-night to her brother.

She trailed upstairs after the other girls. She had just reached the landing when there was a scream, and Lily threw herself into Marguerite's arms.

"What is the matter?" Marguerite gasped, trying to support Lily with one hand and clutching at the banisters with the other.

"It was not you then," Lily muttered. "I should have known it couldn't be you because of the heels."

"What heels? I have no idea what you are talking about." Marguerite was beginning to feel frightened, though she did not know why.

"I must sit down." Lily sank onto the top step and pulled Marguerite down beside her. "I was going along the corridor to my room when I heard steps behind me. I was sure it was you because you stayed downstairs with your brother while the rest of us went up. I only wondered why you were wearing shoes with heels." She looked down at her own flat slippers of soft blue leather with blue tie ribbons matching her silk sash.

"Didn't you look to see who it was?" Marguerite's heart began to flutter.

"Yes—no. . . . That is the frightening part." Lily grasped her hand. "I did turn around, but I did not see anyone. Yet those tap-tap heels went right past me, and I could even hear the rustle of skirts—*silk* skirts. That is strange, now that I think about it. None of us were wearing silk tonight. We were all dressed in white muslin."

Marguerite shivered. "Are you sure there was no one? It is very dark in the corridor."

"I am sure. I had my candle with me, and that lamp on the landing lights up part of the corridor. I don't even know where I dropped that candle. Oh, yes! I remember something else. As the steps passed me, I smelled perfume, something like roses, and yet not roses."

That is exactly what I smelled in my room this morning, Marguerite thought, her throat tight with fear. "Why not tell Mademoiselle Malvina about it?"

"No. I would much rather write to my father and ask him to take me home. But what is the use?" Lily began to wring her hands. "My stepmother will simply tell him that I am imagining things, that I am spoiled, that I want to draw attention to myself."

"Did she ever say anything like that about you?"

"Not really, but she will. I know she will!" Lily began to sob into her handkerchief.

Perhaps she is imagining it all, Marguerite thought. But she described the smell of that perfume exactly as I remember it. She felt the headache grip her temples again and rose. "Come," she said, pulling Lily up by the arm. "Let's go to bed. Maybe we shall both feel better in the morning."

7

The Hollow Tree

But when Marguerite woke up the next morning, she did not feel any better. Squinting, she raised her heavy head from her pillow and let it drop back immediately.

"It is a migraine," Mademoiselle Vanda declared when she came upstairs. "You must stay in bed until it is better. There is a picnic today, but Mademoiselle is not going. She will take good care of you."

Marguerite listened drowsily, wishing that Mademoiselle Vanda would stop talking and go away.

"Please let me sleep," she told the girls who kept tiptoeing in and out of her room, asking how she was feeling. "Mademoiselle is brewing me some tisane and I shall probably be well by the time you are back."

The picnic party left around ten. "In the big carriage," Mademoiselle explained, shuffling around the room with a cup of tisane in her hands. "The young gentleman went on horseback." She held out the cup. "Here, drink this, dear child. It is mint. I put in some honey to make it sweet and just a pinch of other herbs."

Marguerite eyed the pale green liquid with misgiving. She took a cautious sip and found it surprisingly refreshing. Soon the throbbing pain in her temples became fainter and her throat did not feel so dry anymore. She went on sipping slowly. Mademoiselle had collapsed into an armchair by the bed and seemed to be talking to herself.

"Olga liked my mint tisane," she mumbled. "Always asked me for it when she had a migraine headache, and she had them often. Jealousy . . . that is what brought on those attacks. Terrible feeling, jealousy. . . . Makes people stoop to anything, even to crime. . . . Poor little Yani. She was not really pretty, but she had so much charm . . . and heartwarming charm it was."

Marguerite finished her tisane. She was aware that Mademoiselle was still talking, but she was too sleepy to care. With an effort, she managed to put her cup on the bedside table. From somewhere in the back of her mind a question surged: Who was Olga? And Yani? But her eyes were closing in spite of herself. The last words of Mademoiselle floated to her. "That parrot! The minute he saw Yani, he would scream, 'She is ugly! Ugly!' Olga taught him, of course. 'That is cruel,' I told her. . . ."

Marguerite did not hear any more. She was asleep.

She woke up almost three hours later, her headache gone. Hardly daring to believe it, she sat up in bed. Yes, there was no more pain.

Suddenly remembering Mademoiselle, Marguerite looked around. The elderly woman was sitting by the window, her knitting in her lap, her head on her chest, snoring slightly.

Moving cautiously, Marguerite slid out of bed and began to dress. It was wonderful to feel so refreshed and ready for anything. She wondered if she should go downstairs and have something to eat. Her clock showed past one, but somehow the idea of food did not appeal to her. Later, she decided, donning a blue voile dress and tying the ribbons of her shoes. The best thing to do now would be to take a walk and gain some appetite.

She was adjusting her wide-brimmed hat in front of the mirror when it occurred to her that Mademoiselle might wake up and become anxious at finding her gone. Marguerite scribbled a note and pinned it to Mademoiselle's knitting.

It did not surprise her to find the house deserted. The servants were probably having their dinner and taking a long time about it since Malvina was away. Marguerite passed through the hall and went out onto the terrace. It was fun to be alone for once, instead of being surrounded by a crowd of girls. But where to go? She already knew every path of the park. Why not visit the apiary?—not going anywhere near the beehives, of course.

After some thought, Marguerite decided not to go through the park, but to use the shortcut Erast had often mentioned. She turned the corner of the house, skirted the oak tree with its circular bench, and opened the gate that led into a small vegetable garden maintained by the cook. The afternoon was warm. Picking her way between beds of carrots and cabbages, Marguerite felt the sun on her bare arms and was sorry she had not brought along her parasol.

Beyond the vegetable garden, and just across the entrance to the backyard, the path widened and became an avenue lined with trees on the left. On the right stretched lichen-covered walls of low brick buildings, which Marguerite guessed were abandoned barns. Through the gaps between the trees she could see grassy meadows, and still farther away the dark line of a road. Shading her eyes from the sun, Marguerite distinguished the stone urn and realized that it was the same road on which the strange woman had appeared.

Walking slowly to avoid tripping in the numerous potholes, Marguerite tried to remember just what Mademoiselle had been talking about that morning. One name emerged in her memory—Yani. It was not a Russian name, but it could come from the Polish name Yanina. What else did Mademoiselle say? Something about a parrot. Marguerite recalled the parrot voice that had awakened her the other day. Was Mademoiselle's parrot the same as hers?

The thought of Mademoiselle made Marguerite feel uneasy. Perhaps she should not have dashed off on such a long walk. The old lady could be awake now and alarmed in spite of the note. But it would be silly to turn back. She would go on, glance at the apiary from a respectful distance, and then return.

Hurrying now, Marguerite followed the wide bend of the avenue and stopped short at the sight of the apiary. She had often accompanied her grandmother on visits to other country estates. Practically every one had an apiary, but the hives usually stood on a clearing in the park, or even in the back of a flower garden. But this . . . She looked again at the thick hedge, several feet high, with a narrow gate in the middle. Was the gate locked? Marguerite decided not to investigate. There was something foreboding about the dark greenery of the hedge from behind which came a low buzzing sound.

For a moment, Marguerite was tempted to complete her walk by cutting across the meadows to the road and returning home through the park, but she dismissed the idea. It would take too long; she was beginning to feel tired, and a pebble in her shoe hurt her foot.

At the same time she became aware of a sudden discomfort

that came not only from fatigue. She was cold—so cold that the tips of her fingers were numb, and there were goose pimples on her arms.

Instinctively, Marguerite looked up. The sky was no longer blue but pale, and distant. The sun had disappeared, and— No, it could not be. It was just an illusion. She looked again. . . . The almost bare tree branches were swaying in the breeze. As she watched, a yellow leaf fluttered in the air, and joined the other leaves covering the ground in a thick, red-gold carpet. The grass in the meadows was dark, as if touched by frosts.

"It can't be. . . ." Marguerite murmured again, shivering.

A gust of wind shook the trees and made the leaves swirl around her. In sudden panic, Marguerite swung around and started to run down the avenue. She stumbled and fell heavily at the foot of a dead tree that she had not noticed before. As she struggled to her feet, she saw a long, narrow hollow in the trunk. Before she had time to take a step, a swarm of wasps emerged from the hollow and enveloped her head and shoulders in a warm, moving, clinging mass.

Screaming loudly, Marguerite fell again, her left leg doubling under her. . . .

8

The Dancing Lesson

"It was nothing but a nightmare," Malvina declared.

Marguerite was safely back in her room, her foot carefully bandaged by Vanda. She shook her head. "I was not asleep."

"It is not always necessary to be asleep to have a nightmare. You were feeling poorly, and it was most unreasonable of you to get up without permission. I am not even mentioning how improper it is for a young lady to wander around the grounds unaccompanied." Without giving Marguerite a chance to say anything in defense, she went on, "You were probably slightly feverish, and something startled you. It could have been a bird or some flying insect. You were frightened and imagined things that never took place. That dead tree, for instance. There is no such tree in the apiary avenue."

"But I saw it! It had a hollow on one side and wasps flew out of it. A whole swarm of them."

At Marguerite's words Vanda paled and dropped the bandage she was holding. It unrolled across the floor to her sister's feet.

Malvina picked up the bandage and began to roll it up with a nervous, jerky movement. "There is no dead tree," she repeated. "You will be able to see for yourself when your ankle is better. I thought it was something much worse when we came back from the picnic and found you on the ground in a dead faint."

"But I saw the wasps come out," Marguerite protested.

"You say you saw the wasps and that they were all over you. But where are the stings, pray?"

There were none. Marguerite whispered to herself, I had no fever and I know that the tree was there. I wish I could prove it to her.

Unexpectedly, this was done for her the very next day. Bored by the long hours spent in her room, Marguerite persuaded her brother to carry her downstairs for afternoon tea.

It was raining outside and the vast dining room was chilly. Marguerite hugged her pink swansdown jacket around her shoulders and shivered. At least the weather had forced Nicolas to join the rest of the family; his presence always made things livelier. Usually, he hoisted himself on a horse and spent the afternoons cantering through the woods. Now he was teasing Mademoiselle. "You must take a ride with me next time. You could sit in front, sidesaddle of course, and—"

"Nicolas, please leave Mademoiselle alone." Malvina turned to Marguerite. "Be careful of your ankle, my dear. Let your brother bring you a footstool."

Mademoiselle's faded eyes stared at Marguerite across the table. "I have not seen you for a long time, *cherie*. Have you been away visiting your family?"

"She has been sick for one day, Mademoiselle," Ada explained, exasperated.

Nicolas rolled his eyes to the ceiling. "Ah, but a day can be an eternity sometimes."

"I have copied my notes on French literature for you to study," Myra told Marguerite. "We read a comedy by Molière this morning."

"*We,*" Irina whispered under her breath and giggled.

Fortunately, Malvina did not hear the giggle. The twins began to tell Marguerite about a trip to Tula that was planned for the end of the week.

"My ankle will never heal in time for that," Marguerite said wistfully. "I wish I'd never even thought of going to the apiary."

Erast, sitting at the other end of the table deep in thought, suddenly looked up. "But you were not planning to actually enter the apiary, mademoiselle? It could be dangerous. Bees often become excited when someone comes close to the hives, and you had a blue gown on, if I remember rightly."

"I was only planning to look from a distance," Marguerite assured him, wondering what the color of her gown had to do with it. "But I never even reached the gate. I only went as far as that dead tree—"

Malvina's voice rose sharply. "I have already explained to you, Marguerite, that there are no dead trees in the apiary avenue."

"Oh, but there is one." Lily's green eyes were full of mischief.

"How do you know?" Pachette asked.

Her twin repeated, "How?"

"Well, I just could not believe that Marguerite imagined it all. So I got up early this morning and went to look. Almost at the end of the avenue, I found a big stump. It took me a while to discover it because it was all covered with moss, but one can see that the center is rotten. So there could easily have been a hollow there, just as Marguerite described."

A slight gasp came from Ada, echoed by Vanda. Mademoiselle put her hand to her ear. The others just stared.

Only Malvina looked triumphant. "Ah, so it was only a stump that you found. I really have no idea what trees grew in that particular spot years ago. However, there is no dead tree in the avenue *now*. There is a difference between the past and the present, my dear."

Nicolas murmured, "Is there?" and chuckled softly into his tea.

From where she sat, Marguerite could see Ada's hands tightly clenched under the table. She unclasped them slowly, and said with a visible effort, "We are going to have a dancing lesson after tea. I thought it would amuse Marguerite to watch. Would you carry her to the ballroom, please?" She looked at Gaston, who jumped up with alacrity.

"Certainly. A dancing lesson, did you say? May I be a pupil too, please?"

An almost sprightly smile suddenly lit Ada's face. "I was planning to ask you to help me teach," she answered.

He murmured, "Deeply honored," and bowed so low that he almost upset his teacup.

When everybody with the exception of Erast was assembled in the ballroom, Malvina made a speech.

"I suppose all of you have heard about a dance called 'the waltz.' It is considered rather daring by some people, but it is becoming fashionable and I have instructed my niece to show you the steps. However, only your parents can decide whether to permit you to dance it in public."

Malvina sat down between Mademoiselle and Nicolas. The girls looked all agog with excitement. Vanda was at the piano, ready to supply the accompaniment.

Gaston immediately bowed in front of Ada. "Mademoiselle, may I have the pleasure?"

She smiled again. "You know how to waltz? This is very nice. We can show these young ladies how it is done."

Marguerite watched Ada dance away with Gaston, their feet gliding lightly on the parquet floor. As they passed her, she caught sight of Ada's face. Her head was tilted back a little and there was a strange, faraway expression in her eyes.

Pachette whispered, "He is holding her by the waist."

"And holding her hand." Myra gasped. Lily only smiled ironically while Irina gaped.

The dance ended. Ada stood for a moment as if in a daze instead of curtsying, but she recovered herself quickly and ordered, "Please pair off, mesdemoiselles, so that we can begin to learn the steps."

Marguerite suppressed a giggle as she saw her brother advance toward Irina. He had barely begun, "May I . . ." when Irina burst out laughing and covered her face with her sleeve, a gesture that always irritated Malvina. With her other hand, she waved Gaston away.

"Don't ask me," she spluttered. "I could never prance like that."

"You don't like dancing, mademoiselle!"

Irina looked surprised. "Who said I don't like dancing? I do, but *real* dancing."

"What do you mean by real dancing?" Ada asked.

"Like this . . ." Irina began to hum softly. Marguerite recognized the tune. It was an old folk dance. At the same time it seemed to her that Irina winked at Gaston. He must have caught the signal for he started to hum, too, and took a step forward. They began to dance, Gaston advancing, Irina retreating, a village lad courting a village maiden.

Vanda, completely bewildered, looked at Nicolas grinning in the background. He looked back at her and nodded. Taking the nod as a command, she began to play the accompaniment.

For once, Irina's badly cut, too-pink dress did not seem to matter. Soft strands of hair waved around her flushed face. With a quick movement, she produced a handkerchief and twirled it in her raised hand.

The tempo became faster and faster. Irina's skirts brushed Marguerite as she flew past, with Gaston close behind.

A few more figures, and the dance ended. Vanda's hands slid off the keys.

Irina was breathing heavily and fanning herself with her handkerchief. Gaston, looking somewhat contrite, apologized, "I am sorry we disrupted the lesson, Mademoiselle Ada."

"The lesson is over." Ada walked to the window and turned her back to the room. Marguerite thought there were tears in her eyes.

"Excellent performance." Nicolas ignored his half sister's displeased look. "I didn't know you could dance folk dances, young man."

Gaston grinned. "Grandmaman used to let me go to the village weddings when I was a boy. That is how I learned."

Myra said, "My sisters and I used to go to the village weddings, too, sometimes. It was fun."

"We never did," Pachette said regretfully. "Mother would not allow it."

Left to herself at the piano, Vanda played a few random chords, then began to sing in a low voice, *"The moon is high and the garden is still. . . ."*

At the first notes of the song, Ada whirled away from the window. "Aunt Vanda!" she whispered, her eyes on the girls. "Don't!"

Conversation stopped and in the sudden silence, a clear young voice sang, *"The moon is high and the garden is still. . . ."* Then everything became quiet again. Only the smell of perfume lingered in the air.

Marguerite recognized it. . . . She felt Gaston's arm around her shoulders.

Vanda, sitting at the piano, was wringing her hands and repeating, "I am sorry. I forgot. I simply forgot."

"Vanda!" Malvina rose from her chair. "Just what are you lamenting about? Nothing has happened. You were singing and the echo repeated your words. It often happens in old houses like this one." She looked at Nicolas. "Don't you agree?"

He bowed his head. "Whatever you say, sister, whatever you say."

Ada clapped her hands. "We will have some more dancing," she announced. "Quadrille, please, Aunt Vanda."

"Do you believe it was only an echo?" Marguerite asked her brother that evening. "I really wonder if I should not write to grandmaman and tell her I would like to come home. But in her last letter she wrote that the poultry girl has caught smallpox, and the gardener's children are sick with it, too."

Gaston answered quickly. "Of course we couldn't go home now. Not with the sickness still around."

Later, when Marguerite was in bed, there was a knock at the door. Ada came in. "I only wanted to find out how your ankle is after your being up for most of the afternoon." She sat down beside the bed.

"I am not tired at all, and my ankle is much less swollen," Marguerite assured her. She realized that Ada was not listening. Her eyes were fixed on the silken ball on the writing desk.

"I think that is the same one," Ada murmured. "Yes, I am sure it is."

"Is it yours?" Marguerite asked eagerly.

Ada shook her head. "No, not really, but I played with it when I was a child." She pressed her hand to her forehead. "It brings back memories. You probably know that I am an orphan. I was only six when my parents died. They were driving back from the theater when the horses became frightened of something, and the coachman could not control them. The carriage overturned, and my parents were killed."

There was a long pause. "And you were sent here?" Marguerite dared to ask at last.

Ada nodded. "Yes, the Astrovs were my closest relatives. I remember the day I arrived from Warsaw, all in black, and holding on tightly to my uncle Nicolas's hand. The minute I stepped into this house, I became afraid of it, even though everybody was nice to me—especially Aunt Vanda. Then, one day, a maid gave me this ball. She explained that she had found it in a cupboard and wanted me to have it because I had hardly any toys. I was playing with it on the terrace when I threw it too far, and it went over the balustrade. I was just going to run down the steps and retrieve it when I saw it sailing through the air toward me, as if someone had thrown it back. I could not believe my eyes, so I tossed the ball over the balustrade again, and again the same thing happened. Then I heard someone laugh, quite close. But when I looked around there was no one. I screamed and ran to my aunt Malvina. But when I sobbed out my story, she became very angry and told me that it was all my imagination, that I was inventing it. When I insisted I was tell-

THE DANCING LESSON

ing the truth, she slapped my face and threatened to punish me severely if I ever 'made a scene' again."

She spoke haltingly. "Later, other things happened—things I could not explain. I never talked about them, but I was frightened, and I am still frightened. . . ."

Ada sat quietly, her hands folded in her lap.

Feeling uncomfortable, Marguerite blurted out, "I enjoyed watching you waltz with my brother today. You danced so beautifully."

"Did I?" Ada's eyes were looking somewhere beyond Marguerite. "I only know that I felt as if I were carried away, far, far from here, and that I was no longer afraid. . . ." The last words were so faint, Marguerite guessed rather than heard them.

Suddenly Ada's expression changed. "I am sorry I talked so much," she said abruptly, rising from her seat, "but sometimes one simply must. Good night, Marguerite." And she left the room.

75

9

Yani

By the end of the week, Marguerite's ankle was quite well again, but Malvina decided it would not be wise for her to go on the shopping trip with the rest of the girls. "It is almost two hours' journey in the carriage, and that is too tiring for you," she declared. "Besides, you might hurt your ankle again on the cobblestones."

The pupils spent an entire evening sitting in the library and drawing up lists of what they intended to buy—toilet water, notepaper, ribbons, perfumed soap, stockings, and garters. . . .

"Just write down what you need and I shall be pleased to shop for you," Myra urged Marguerite.

"I was going to ask Gaston—" Marguerite began.

"No, no, let me do it. Men don't know a thing about ribbons or gloves." She added with a rueful smile, "Besides, it will be fun to buy things, even if they are not for me."

Seeing Marguerite's surprised expression, she explained, "I

have not received any allowance this week. Mama wrote that there was just enough money to pay the mortgage till the end of the year. Things are very difficult at home."

At the other end of the library Lily was saying, "I am going to buy a new hat, with a big feather in front and a small veil. My stepmother said that style was most unsuitable for a young girl, and that is why I am going to buy it. Papa gives me plenty of pocket money."

The party left early the next morning. Sitting on the terrace, Marguerite watched the open carriage being brought to the front of the house.

The pupils, all clutching light shawls over their dresses and doing their best not to drop their parasols and reticules, piled in, followed by Vanda and Ada.

Behind the carriage Gaston was prancing on horseback. He was in high spirits, scaring the elderly coachman out of his wits by calling out to him, "Watch the axle! I can hear it crack. The front wheels? They are almost off."

At last the carriage moved down the avenue, and Gaston cantered after it with a ringing shout of "Onward! Onward!"

Marguerite hoped that Malvina would leave her alone to sit on the shady terrace and read the book her grandmother had sent her. To her dismay, the older woman sat down on one of the cushioned wrought-iron seats and produced knitting from the deep pocket of her gown. "We will have a light meal served in the library since there are so few of us," she told Marguerite. "In the meantime, the maids are turning out the dining-room cupboard, cleaning the silver, and washing the china and crystal."

"Yes, mademoiselle," Marguerite answered, wondering whether it was permissible to pick up her book.

Before she could decide, Malvina asked abruptly, "Is your brother supposed to inherit the estate after your grandmother?"

Any allusion to her grandmother's death always upset Marguerite to the point of tears. To her great relief, Liubasha appeared on the terrace and breathlessly informed Malvina that the big blue dish that was always kept on the top shelf of the cupboard was no longer in its place.

"Oh, no!" Malvina rose. "It is very valuable. I had better see for myself." She walked away with Liubasha, leaving Marguerite in peace.

Instead of reading, Marguerite lay back in her chair, gazing at the sunlit garden and trying to imagine how it looked when the trees and bushes were trimmed and statues rose above the flower beds.

As she looked, it seemed to her that a slight figure in blue lurked for a second in the distant group of trees. Almost at the same time she heard a young voice call, "Palkan! Palkan!" A faint bark answered.

"I am imagining things," Marguerite tried to reassure herself, but her hands trembled as she took up her book.

A shadow fell on the flagstones. Marguerite looked up and saw Lavrentii standing on the terrace steps, looking at her. She suppressed a gesture of annoyance.

"Yes, Lavrentii?" she asked, trying not to sound impatient.

The old man jerked his thumb in the direction of the garden. "Did you hear?"

Marguerite nodded.

"Ah, so you did? I heard it too. I thought I was going to see Little Yani and her dog run down the path."

"Little Yani?" Marguerite thought of Mademoiselle's ramblings.

"You don't know about her?" Groaning, Lavrentii lowered

himself onto the top step, leaned against the balustrade, and closed his eyes.

Marguerite watched him uneasily, thinking that he was going to sleep. Suddenly his sunken eyes fixed on her again.

"Was just trying to remember the year the mistress died," he muttered. "1761 it was. The younger boy was only five, the older ten, and I was not much older."

Nicolas and Erast, Marguerite interpreted in her mind.

"The master grieved terrible. Packed up and went to Warsaw. Had some big post there. The tsar gave it to him. Stayed away two years, so Mamzelle was in charge of the house."

"Mademoiselle?" Marguerite asked quickly. "*Our* Mademoiselle?"

"Same one." Lavrentii looked disdainful. "And a giddy young thing she was. Used to play games with the two older children."

"Olga?" Her grandmother had said Nicolas and Erast had an older sister.

"That is right." Lavrentii nodded. "And there was the young Alexander. Not that he was the master's son. Just a poor relative. His parents had too many children, twelve of them. So the master took one of the boys and brought him up as his own. A handsome fellow he was, and gay, but not much here." The old butler tapped his forehead. "He was fourteen at that time and Olga thirteen, but she behaved like she was the mistress of the house. Servants came to her for orders—were afraid of her, too." He chuckled.

"Was she beautiful?"

Lavrentii shrugged his shoulders. "Beautiful? I suppose you could call her that. Dark— Eh, what is there for me to say when you can see her every day."

"Ada! Of course, she is Olga's granddaughter."

Lavrentii nodded and started to say something, but instead went into a fit of coughing. When it was over, he pocketed his big handkerchief and continued with a slight wheezing, "So Olga was not very happy when a letter came from Warsaw, saying that the master had married a Polish woman and was coming home with his new wife. She and Alexander had got used to running wild all over the estate during those two years. Mamzelle had no authority over them, really. Olga was afraid they might both be sent to boarding schools. But nothing like that happened. The Polish woman was easygoing and a kindly soul. Both Olga and Alexander soon became fond of her. Not that she had much time for them, mind you. Less than a year after she arrived at Astrovo a girl was born, and about two years later the other one."

Malvina and Vanda, Marguerite whispered to herself.

"The master hired a tutor for Alexander," Lavrentii went on. "That was all. Nothing was changed much. But then . . . Yani came."

Marguerite looked at the group of trees from where the voice had come. "Yani? But who was she?"

"The new mistress's younger sister. Just come out of school, convent school they called it. Somewhere near Warsaw. Her real name was Yanina, but she liked to be called Yani and the name suited her. She was so slender and childlike. The servants called her Little Yani among themselves. Can't say she was pretty—small, round face and a wide mouth. Brown eyes and brown hair. Just a mop of curls, but every curl seemed to dance. And kind! She made friends with everybody. Knew every servant as if they were relatives. Asked about their families in the village, sent gifts to their children. And the horses! Her pockets were always full of bread and lumps of sugar for them. There was an old dog chained in the backyard in those times; Palkan was his name. The very first day Yani came, she had him untied and he followed her everywhere. But one person she could not make friends with."

"Olga."

"Olga." Lavrentii sighed. "She hated Yani. Said she was too familiar with people who were not of her class and that it was silly and childish of her to always sing and play ball in the park. But that was not the real reason; the real reason was Alexander. He was brought up with Olga and to her he was like a brother. But when she saw him walk in the garden with Yani, rush to help Yani into the saddle when she went riding . . . well, she must have realized he was more than a brother to her. This made her hate Yani even more, and she did her best to annoy her in every way. Once, just before a ball, she upset some ink on Yani's gown. Pretended it happened by accident. Then she found another way. Taught her parrot, a big blue-and-yellow bird, to scream 'She is ugly!' the minute Yani entered the room."

"But were Alexander and Yani really in love, or did Olga only imagine it?" Marguerite wondered.

"Oh, they loved each other well enough. Only Alexander was a weakling, see. He kept putting off telling Olga he loved Yani and intended to marry her. Instead, he pretended there was nothing between them when Olga was around. But she was not only beautiful, she was shrewd, too, and she watched the two of them.

"And so it went on for a few months." Lavrentii's voice became tense with emotion. "Then Olga's eighteenth birthday came around. There was to be a big celebration at Astrovo. People came from all over the county. The ballroom was full of hothouse flowers; ladies were all feathers and diamonds. It was a beautiful sight! A military orchestra was playing and everybody was dancing. I was a young lad then, just turned nineteen and trained to be a footman."

Lavrentii straightened up. "The butler sent me to bring some flowers for the dining-room table. That was when I saw Olga slip into the music room."

Seeing Marguerite's puzzled look, he explained, "In those days there was another room beyond the library, with a spinet in it and a harp. Later, when there was a fire at Astrovo, the music room was burned down. I was away at the time, so I don't know exactly how it happened. Seems that someone upset a candelabra and the draperies caught fire. Anyway, the music room was never rebuilt, which is why the left wing is shorter than the right one."

"Never mind that. What happened in the music room? Did you see?"

"That I did. All the servants were gossiping about them, so I got curious. I followed her and watched from behind the door. Alexander was in there with Yani in his arms. Olga did not say a word when she saw them. She just stood there, breaking her fan to pieces. Then she turned around and walked out. Those two never even noticed her. Sure enough, I blabbed to the other servants about what I saw and we all waited to see what Olga would do. Nothing happened the next day, but the day after, Olga waylaid one of the maids. She ordered her to tell Yani that Alexander had left a letter for her in the hollow of the dead tree at the end of the avenue that leads to the beehives. Then she gave the maid a little necklace with a locket and made her swear that she would not reveal to Yani the message came through her—Olga, that is."

"I know that tree," Marguerite whispered. "I saw it. Wasps came from the hollow."

Lavrentii peered at her. "You saw it? I thought you might

have. Yes, there was a wasps' nest in that hollow. I saw them buzzing around in summer. Naturally, they were asleep in November. Was it November? Yes, sure enough. Olga's birthday was on the eleventh, so this must have happened on the thirteenth—or was it fourteenth? I don't remember."

"Did Yani go?"

"Eh, no, it did not happen that way." Lavrentii bit his lip. "The maid was new in the house, fresh from the village she was. After Olga talked to her, she became all excited and confused. So she told Alexander that Yani had left a letter for *him* in that tree. He went immediately, and not knowing about the nest he put his hand right into the hollow. The wasps swarmed all over him. They don't like to be disturbed. The housekeeper happened to be coming from the village at that time. She saw Alexander on the ground, all covered with wasps, and ran down the road, screaming for help. The gardener and his two assistants were pruning trees on the edge of the park, right by that stone urn. They heard the housekeeper's screams and rushed to rescue Alexander, but it was too late."

"He died! I did not know one could die of wasps' stings."

"Some people do and some don't," Lavrentii answered knowingly. "When poison from stings gets into the blood one never knows what can happen. Alexander died soon after he was brought into the house."

"And Olga? What did she say when she saw Alexander dying?"

"Olga?" Lavrentii thought it over. "Nothing. She just stood there and stared as if she were of stone. Stayed that way, too. I mean, she spoke and moved around, but there was no more life in her than in Alexander."

"And no one knew she caused his death!" Marguerite exclaimed indignantly.

"Who said nobody knew? The maid got hysterical when she saw what had happened, and she sobbed out the whole story, about how Olga had bribed her to give the message to Yani and how she had got it all wrong. Not that Olga cared whether people knew or not. Anyway, pretty soon the master took the whole family abroad and they stayed there for about three years. Olga never came back. She married a Polish nobleman and settled in Warsaw. She was in her late thirties when she died. Had an only daughter, Ada's mother."

"And Yani?" Marguerite's throat was tight.

Lavrentii looked away for a moment. "Yani . . . poor soul. She blamed herself for not saving Alexander. Seems that she was in the music room when he went to that hollow tree. He passed under the windows and she saw him. It looked strange to her that he was out for a walk in such damp, windy weather. She was going to open the window and call him. If she had, he would probably have told her about the message he'd received and everything would have been cleared up. Only she did not open that window because it was cold outside and she had on a light gown. She let him go by. . . .

"When he died, something dimmed in her mind. She would stand by that same window for hours, tapping on the glass and calling, 'Alexander! Alexander!' Or she would wander around the park, all pale and wasted, still calling and never getting an answer. The dog would run after her, whimpering and licking her hands. Ah, it was a pitiful sight. Finally, the mistress arranged for some relatives to come and take her away to Poland. It was thought that a change would be good for her. But she kept getting weaker and one day she went to sleep. . . . Never woke up."

"And the dog?"

"He howled for days after Yani left. Then one day I came out and there he was, stretched on the garden path, dead. We found out later it happened on the same day Little Yani died. Perhaps she called him and he heard." The old man suddenly raised his hand.

Once again, a faint "Palkan!" came from the depths of the garden.

Marguerite started.

Lavrentii eyed her sternly. "It is no use getting yourself all worked up. An evil deed has been done and a poor innocent soul paid for it. No wonder it can't rest in peace." Still mumbling something, he heaved himself up and shuffled down the terrace steps.

Just then Malvina appeared. "I hope he was not annoying you with his old stories, my dear," she said. "He is getting old and gets obsessed with his . . . let's call them vagaries . . . more and more often. I was looking for that blue dish. I can't imagine how it could have disappeared."

She went on talking, but Marguerite was not listening. In her mind, she was following Yani along the garden paths. . . .

10

The Peacock Shawl

The girls returned about four in the afternoon. Marguerite watched them from her bedroom window. The coachman carried a load of packages, including two pink-and-white striped hatboxes, into the house. So Lily must have bought a hat as she planned, Marguerite thought, and someone else must have bought one too. Gaston was not in sight.

Soon footsteps ran up the stairway, doors opened and closed, and Liubasha rushed along the corridor with pitchers of warm water.

Since it was almost teatime, Marguerite decided to go to the dining room and wait there for her companions. As she approached the dining-room door, she heard Malvina and Vanda talking inside. Uncertain whether she should enter or wait in the hall, Marguerite stopped. Vanda's voice, high-pitched and annoyed, floated through the half-opened door. "A most tiring trip. The roads were extremely dusty, and the girls chattered so much. As to the young count, he behaved in a very objection-able manner."

"Really?" Malvina sounded skeptical.

"Judge for yourself. As we were driving through the village, he somehow spread word among the peasants that this was a wedding. Within a few minutes a whole crowd had collected. We could hardly pass through. Then the sexton arrived wring-ing his hands because the priest was away for the day and could not perform the ceremony. It took me quite a while to calm him down. Later, the count insisted we take a shortcut, which turned out to be a bridge so rickety the carriage was swaying like a boat. The girls screamed, and I felt uneasy too. Don't smile, Malvina. It was very frightening. Wait until you hear the rest."

Marguerite froze in her place.

"We went to the milliner's because Lily wanted to buy a hat," Vanda went on in the same offended tone. "Ada needed one too. Her bonnet was getting too shabby. I selected a very nice one for her, plain white straw with a blue ribbon. Modest and inexpensive. All of a sudden, the young man reaches out and picks another bonnet from the counter, a most extravagant one, pink, with a big pink rose in front. He insisted that Ada try it on. He actually threatened, jokingly I hope, that if she did not comply, he would lay himself across the door of the shop and would not let her out."

"And did she try the hat?" Malvina sounded amused.

"She bought it."

For the first time since her arrival at Astrovo, Marguerite heard Malvina laugh. It was not unpleasant laughter; hearty and throaty, it sounded like a man's.

Vanda said, "I am glad you find it amusing. But you have not heard yet what happened in the next shop we went to. It was that big one under the arcades."

"I know it. Go on."

"They had nice shawls and Irina liked one very much. It was really lovely, a peacock pattern in beautiful blue and a nice light silk, just right for the summer. But it was very expensive and I was sure she would not buy it. Not that girl! She began to *bargain* instead. First she pretended to leave the shop, then she told the salesman that the material was too thin, that a thread was pulled in one corner, that the color would wear out fast. He defended his merchandise, but for every word he said, she had ten."

"She must have learned how to bargain in her father's store."

"I should hope not in this house. People were staring at us. A well-dressed young girl with a chaperon *bargaining*. The young count enjoyed it immensely. He kept encouraging her and even offered her his arm when she pretended to leave the store. She finally succeeded in getting the shawl at half price, and he called 'Bravo!' "

Marguerite suddenly realized she was eavesdropping and moved noiselessly away from the door. Trying to step as lightly as possible, she moved across the hall toward the terrace. As she passed the drawing-room door she saw Ada standing in front of the big mirror, tying the ribbons of her new bonnet.

For a second, Marguerite wondered whether the flushed, smiling face framed in pink ruching, with the rose nestling above the shiny dark waves of hair, could be Ada's. It seemed to her that the girl in the pink bonnet was asking herself the same question.

11

At the Stables

June came, unusually hot and with frequent thunderstorms. There were two more picnics, and a moonlit walk in the park to admire the glowworms. Erast kept rubbing his hands and saying that the bees were laying away a good supply of honey. Nicolas's gout was so much better, he started to give riding lessons with Gaston as assistant. Shouts of laughter mingled with screams from Irina, who loved horses but was afraid to sit on one, came from the stables.

Marguerite dutifully took part in all the amusements, but secretly she preferred to be alone. The story of Yani fascinated her, and she wished she could find out more about her. After some rummaging in the library, she found a pile of old magazines, *Les Modes*, most of them dating back to the 1760s. What kind of gown would Yani be wearing? Marguerite wondered, turning the yellowed pages. At last she found a gown that would suit Yani perfectly: white dimity, with embroidery of forget-me-nots. Now she could see her clearly, her slender waist rising above the big side hoops, panniers, her small hands throwing the silken ball for Palkan to catch. Would Yani powder her hair? For big balls, yes, but otherwise she would probably tie back her curls with a snood . . . a blue snood to match the forget-me-nots.

Olga would have her hair dressed high and held at top with a small gilded comb as in one of the pictures in the magazine. Marguerite dressed her in vivid green silk with cascades of white lace at the throat and on the sleeves. Alexander . . . there were no men's fashions in *Les Modes*, so she had to content herself by imagining him in short breeches and long silk stockings, and a dark blue jacket embroidered on the front. His hair was rather long and combed back, held with a bow at the nape. . . .

It was fun dressing the three people who had lived at Astrovo sixty years ago, assigning rooms to them, finding out what books they were likely to read. But as they became more real, Marguerite began to feel frightened. Somehow, Olga's face took on Ada's features, Alexander's laughing eyes became those of Gaston, Yani . . . Marguerite began to laugh. No, Irina was not at all like Yani and certainly no one was trying to kill her.

She was thinking about it again the next morning while standing on the terrace. Her thoughts were interrupted by Irina, who rushed up the terrace steps, pale and shaking. "Prince almost killed me just now."

"Prince?" Marguerite asked. "Oh, the horse! How? Did you try to ride him?"

Irina shook her head. "Oh, no! I just went to give some goodies to the horses, as I do every morning. I had some carrots for

Prince and bread for the rest. Prince loves carrots, but this time something must have been wrong with them. He had barely started to chew when his eyes began to roll, and he whinnied and started to kick. I bent down to pick up the empty basket, and his hoof missed my temple by a hairbreadth. I screamed, and a groom came. He patted Prince and calmed him down. I told him what had happened and he said that something must have been wrong with the carrots."

"But what could be wrong?" Marguerite asked. "And how could Prince kick so high if he were in his stall?"

Irina looked startled. "In the stall? No! All the horses are out in the yard at this hour of the morning. They are tethered to the wall while the stables are being cleaned. You must have seen those big iron rings."

Marguerite shuddered. "I see now. You could have been killed or crippled. A frightened horse can kick hard. . . . Are you going to tell Mademoiselle Malvina about it?"

"Never. She might stop me from going to the stables again." Suddenly, Irina turned her head. "What do you want?" she asked as Lily appeared noiselessly at her side.

Lily's eyes were bright with curiosity. "Didn't you say you almost had an accident at the stables?" she asked. Having broached the subject, she went on glibly, "You leave your basket in the pantry every evening, don't you? So the cook can fill it for you."

Irina nodded grudgingly.

"That means anyone could meddle with the basket," Lily went on. "May I?" She leaned forward and taking the basket from Irina's lap began to examine it, holding it to the light and even sniffing it.

Why does she like to snoop so much? Marguerite wondered. Perhaps it takes her mind off brooding over her stepmother.

Walking to the terrace balustrade, Lily spread her handkerchief on its flat top and began to shake the basket over it. "Come and look!" she called triumphantly to the girls.

"What is that?" Irina asked, staring at several red grains sticking to the white linen. She touched them gingerly with her finger, then put her finger in her mouth. "Hot red pepper!"

Lily gloated. "I saw something red sticking between the wickerwork," she explained. "It must have stung Prince's mouth terribly. No wonder he started to kick."

"But why didn't I see it?" Irina faltered, staring at the basket.

"You would have, if it were on the bread. It wouldn't be noticeable on the carrots, especially if there was any greenery on them."

Irina nodded. "There was. But where would one get red pepper? Spices are expensive. I know because Papasha had them in his store."

Marguerite said reluctantly, "There is a spice cupboard in the pantry. Ada is in charge of it. I saw her once unlock it and give some cinnamon to the cook."

"But Ada wouldn't play such a silly joke on me."

It may not have been a joke, flashed through Marguerite's mind. She said, "Maybe Ada simply upset some red pepper over your basket. It could happen."

Irina welcomed this suggestion. "Of course! It could easily happen in a pantry. Let's not talk about it, not even among ourselves. Shall we?" Her honest blue eyes went from Marguerite's to Lily's face.

"Very well." There seemed to be nothing else to say. Lily only shrugged her shoulders.

The girls were just turning to go inside when there was a gay "Good morning, ladies!" Gaston appeared on the terrace. He bowed to Irina and Lily, and waved a sheet of paper in his sister's direction. "A letter from grandmaman," he announced. "The messenger has just arrived. Good news!"

Marguerite's companions discreetly withdrew, leaving her alone with her brother. He threw his arm around Marguerite's shoulders and leaned on the balustrade beside her.

"Good news," he repeated. "Guess what."

"Grandmaman wants you to return home," Marguerite answered quickly.

Gaston grinned. "Wrong! She *was* going to order me home. There are no fresh cases of smallpox and everything has been washed, scrubbed, and fumigated. However, she has received a letter from Mademoiselle Malvina, who wrote that I am such a charming, well-mannered, intelligent young man and such a wonderful companion to your fellow pupils, she would like me to prolong my visit for a few more weeks. Grandmaman said yes. She is giving me till August the first. Then I simply must go home and start cramming for my entrance examination. Now, isn't it wonderful?"

Marguerite did not answer. Her brother gave her a keen look. "You don't seem to be pleased at the idea of my staying here."

Marguerite's lips began to tremble. "I do want you to stay," she whispered, "and yet . . . I am afraid."

"You are afraid? What of?"

Marguerite looked around to make sure they were alone. "Listen," she whispered. "Remember the day you all went shopping in Tula? Lavrentii came and talked to me." She began to tell Gaston the story of Yani.

He listened attentively, but to Marguerite's irritation, by the time she reached the end of the story he was smiling.

Ignoring the smile, Marguerite told him about the incident at
the stables. "Please don't make fun of it, Gaston. Don't you see
now why I am afraid?"

He laughed outright. "You are afraid that the story might
repeat itself? Surely you don't believe Lavrentii's stories! He is
so old he simply doesn't realize where the truth ends and fairy
tales begin."

"He could not have invented all those people," Marguerite
protested. "They must have existed."

"Of course they existed. But whatever happened to them was
much more ordinary than Lavrentii made you believe. Probably
that girl—what is her name?—Yani, flirted a little with the handsome Alexander and the other girl was jealous. That is only
natural. Servants knew about the situation and enjoyed blow-
ing every small happening into a big, dramatic event. No one
tried to kill anyone, you may be sure of it. As to Alexander, he
must have seen something unusual about that hollow tree and
decided to investigate. Silly of him to thrust his hand into the
hollow, but he evidently did not know about the wasps' nest."

"He died from the stings," Marguerite reminded him.

"That could happen. Some people can't stand the poison of
insects. You were too small to remember, but grandmaman had
a coachman who was stung by a bumblebee. He died on the
spot."

"And Irina?"

"Irina should know better than to come so close to a horse,
especially when the animal is not in its stall."

"And the red pepper?" Marguerite insisted.

"Had nothing to do with it. The horse simply got scared of
something. They do. The pepper just happened to fall into the
basket. A few grains! I know that spice cupboard. It smells . . .
mmm." Gaston raised his eyes to heaven. "I saw Mademoiselle

Ada take out some vanilla for a dessert yesterday. She was going to make it with her own hands too. Pretty hands she has, don't you think?"

"I have not noticed her hands," Marguerite answered. "I wish you would be serious."

"Oh, but I am! Do you know that her eyes can laugh, but she does not permit her lips to laugh too. I wish I had some magic potion to make her gayer, warmer, not so grave, a little less pale maybe. . . ."

"And Irina?" Marguerite asked ironically. "What would you change about her?"

"Irina? I would make her more slender and her face a little less round, but I would leave her eyes and hair alone. But no!" he suddenly exclaimed. "On second thought, I would not change anything about *her.*"

"I see." For the first time in her life, Marguerite felt that in some ways she was older than her brother.

He patted her hand. "You sound like Mademoiselle Malvina. Do smile, and forget Lavrentii's nonsense."

Marguerite remained grave. "I heard Yani's voice."

"Because that old fool persuaded you that you did. Let's go to breakfast now." He took her arm. "Think about the wonderful time we shall all have this summer. And please believe me that nothing bad is going to happen."

"Nothing bad is going to happen," Marguerite said as she extinguished her candle that night. For a few minutes she felt comforted; but when the darkness closed around her bed, she became frightened again.

12

In the Apiary

Next morning dawned hot and humid. Both windows in the library were wide open. The pupils languished through German literature and geography. History with Nicolas was supposed to be the next lesson, but he suddenly revolted.

"No and no!" he shouted just outside the library door. "I am not going to talk about Ancient Greece in this heat. I am going for a good canter in the woods before lunch. The young ladies can go on expecting me. What about using Erast? Surely he must know something about Ancient Greece. After all, he went to school too."

Heavy steps sounded in the corridor, followed by Ada's light tread. She reappeared in the library after a short while, and announced that instead of a history lesson they were going to visit the apiary and learn how bees made honey.

"I am sure it will be most instructive," Myra told Marguerite as they were going outside.

"I suppose so," Marguerite answered, her eyes on Myra's pale, drawn face. "Should you go? It is quite a long walk and you look poorly."

Myra sighed. "No, I am not poorly. I had an upsetting letter from home. My two little sisters are both sick with measles. This means a doctor, medicines, and there is no money. I am—" She suddenly broke off and staring at the library window whispered, "Did you see someone waving?"

The girls with Ada at their head were just turning the corner of the house. Marguerite looked back quickly. She was just in time to see a small hand waving through the window. The next minute it was gone.

Yani? For Myra's benefit, Marguerite said, "It was only the sun reflecting in the windowpane."

Myra gave her a hard look. "It was not the sun. And I am sure this is not the first strange thing you have seen here. But you are right to keep quiet. Mademoiselle Malvina could say we have 'nerves' and send us home. I want to stay and learn all I can. Don't you think it is wise?"

"I don't know," Marguerite answered in all sincerity as they hurried to catch up with the others.

It turned out to be a pleasant walk. Lily grumbled that it was too hot, but the other girls agreed that it was nice to walk under the trees and feel the breeze on their faces.

Marguerite dreaded passing the place where she had seen the hollow tree, but the stump was not visible in the grass.

The apiary was bigger than she had expected, a long, narrow, green meadow surrounded by flowering bushes and enclosed by a tall hedge. At the far end stood a low building of rough stone. Erast emerged from the door, looking not unlike a bee himself in his brown jacket and tight black trousers. A white scarf around his neck almost reached his ears. The bees had a special liking for stinging him on the neck, he explained to the girls.

This explanation did not reassure the pupils, who stood in a tight group, eyeing the six hives standing in two rows on the grass. The unexpected arrival of Gaston, who came sliding in through the gate, was greeted with exclamations of joy.

"I followed you all the way, creeping along, and you never saw me," he announced triumphantly. "Are we going to eat honey?"

Erast smiled. "It is too early for honey, young man."

"We came here to learn something about the ways of bees," Ada explained.

"I am a pupil too, then." Gaston joined the group and stood beside Marguerite.

"I think, Uncle Erast, the pupils would be especially interested in your African bees," Ada said, nodding at a big glass hive standing a good distance away from the others.

Erast frowned. "I don't think it would be wise, my dear. In order to see anything, you would all have to come close and this might irritate the bees." He turned to the girls. "You see those bees? They are from Africa. A sailor brought me a few, and I succeeded in getting them used to our climate. Their honey is superior to that of our bees and they produce more of it. But they have a very mean temper. Perhaps it is because the Africans are constantly hunting for their nests to get the honey. They became real man-haters and they attack to kill."

"Do they have more poison than the other bees?" Myra asked timidly.

Erast began to explain eagerly, "No, mademoiselle. The African bee's sting is no worse than that of any other breed. But they get excited much more easily and then they get in what is commonly known as a 'stinging frenzy.' If provoked, two or three hundred African bees might sting in one minute, but only ten of our own bees. Many Africans are killed trying to rob a nest."

The girls looked impressed. Myra wrote furiously in her notebook.

"Please follow me, mesdemoiselles," Erast said. "We can look at those other hives. They are quite safe."

There were little squeals of fear as a bee flew past, but everybody soon became fascinated by Erast's story of how honey was made and about the swarms.

A bee alighted on Ada's sleeve. She jerked back. Erast raised his hand, and she froze in her place. The bee promptly flew away, a brown streak in the air.

"You see," Erast said, "our native bees are really peace-loving. If you don't slap at them or otherwise disturb them, they simply leave you alone."

Lily glanced at Marguerite. "But they do attack if disturbed, and wasps would do the same."

"Certainly, mademoiselle." Erast nodded. "I know a few cases. Right here, about sixty years ago—"

"Uncle Erast," Ada interrupted sharply, "I am afraid we have already taken up too much of your time. It has been most interesting but we must go back now."

"Give me a few more minutes, Ada." He addressed the girls. "Young ladies, I have experimented with both the African and our native bees and came to the conclusion that they can distinguish colors. I put two dishes by the hives, a white one containing ordinary water and a blue one with sugared water. In a few days, I noticed that the bees flew straight to the dish containing sugar. Let me show you. . . ." He disappeared into the stone building and came out a few minutes later with a very ordinary white dish in one hand and a beautiful blue one in the other.

"That is the dish Aunt Malvina said had disappeared!" Ada exclaimed. "It is very valuable. And you had it all this time."

"Valuable?" Erast stared at the dish as if he was seeing it for the first time. "I had no idea Malvina was looking for it."

"Why did you take this one? There are plenty of ordinary blue dishes."

"It was just the right shade, very distinctive," Erast answered simply. Ada burst into a gay, ringing laugh.

Erast mumbled, "I had better wash the thing and return it," and fled inside.

Ada laughed again and turned to go. Her head brushed a flowering branch of a tree and a shower of petals descended on her hair. "Oh," she exclaimed, flicking the petals off.

Gaston rushed up to her. "No, please! Leave a few. They suit you so well. Just these on the temples."

"Very well." Smiling, she fluffed the curls with the yellow petals clinging to them. "How does it look now?" she asked.

"Marvelous." Together they moved toward the gate, the girls after them.

There was a sudden, muffled scream from Irina. A bee was entangled in the long fringe of her peacock shawl. Buzzing angrily, it tried to free itself but only became more and more entangled in the silk threads.

"It is going to sting me!" Irina cried, and flung herself against Gaston. "Take it off! Take it off!"

He jerked the shawl off Irina's shoulders and shook it vigorously. The released bee flew off and vanished in the bushes.

"Thank you."

"But you said you were not afraid of bees," Gaston teased, draping the shawl around Irina's shoulders.

Ada said, "You should show more restraint, Irina. There was no need for that screaming. After all, you were not stung—or were you?"

"Stung? If I were I would scream louder than that. What was I supposed to do? Scream in French to make it ladylike?"

Ada did not answer and the other pupils pretended not to hear. The small procession resumed its way toward the gate. It was Irina who now walked at Gaston's side; Ada followed with the others, her face pale and set.

13

Hide-and-Seek

The visit to the apiary was barely over when the sky became cloudy and from far away there came a rumble of thunder. The girls hurried into the house, but nothing happened. The heat only became more oppressive, making everybody feel tired and out of sorts. Even Gaston did not talk and joke as usual.

Darkness brought some freshness to the air. The entire Astrov family and the pupils gathered on the terrace, watching the distant flashes of lightning above the treetops.

Marguerite stood leaning on the balustrade of the terrace. "Thunderstorm, but several miles away," Nicolas's voice said behind her. He came closer and gazed at the sky. "There is a circle around the moon," he remarked. "That is a sure sign that there will be a change in the weather."

Mademoiselle joined them, looking more haggard than usual, gray hair hanging in wisps from under her tulle cap. "What did you say about the moon?" she asked Nicolas, and without waiting for his answer went on, "Ah, when I first came here the grounds looked different. There were flowers everywhere. We liked to play hide-and-seek on moonlit nights, the children and I. I felt like a child myself. After all, I was only nineteen. But then . . . time went so fast, and all at once they were not children anymore. . . ." Suddenly she became quiet, gazing with strange intensity into space.

Marguerite held her breath. Vanda had said once that there were times when the old governess, who could not recall the day before, went back into her memories and seemed to remember every detail. "She acts then as if past were present," Vanda explained.

Nicolas was evidently expecting something to happen, too, for his eyes were fixed on Mademoiselle's shadowy figure.

Suddenly, it came. Mademoiselle threw back her head and called in a voice that held a ring of youth, "Olga! Alexander! The moon is high. Let's play hide-and-seek. Where is Yani? Fetch her, Alexander. It is no use sulking, Olga. The more of us, the merrier. I am going to hide first and I dare you to find me. Oh, I forgot! It is forbidden to hide in the gardener's cellar. The steps are too steep, one can get hurt. But we can . . ."

Her voice sank so low, Marguerite could not distinguish the words. Nicolas touched her shoulder. "Don't disturb her," he whispered. "She is going to doze now." Taking the elderly woman's arm, he gently led her to the nearest seat. She sank into it, still mumbling, but soon she became quiet, breathing evenly and apparently fast asleep.

Vanda said with relief, "It is over. Now she will sleep for at least a couple of hours and when she wakes up she won't remember anything."

"You don't have to whisper, young ladies," Malvina said. "She won't hear you, even if you shouted into her ear."

Pachette exclaimed, "Hide-and-seek in the moonlight! What a wonderful idea. May we, please, Mademoiselle Ada?"

"I really don't know—" Ada began.

Malvina broke in. "You certainly may, Pachette. I am sure everybody is going to enjoy it. But please, not in the park. Stay as close to the house as possible."

The announcement was greeted by a chorus of joyful exclamations. The girls, led by Gaston, tripped down the terrace steps.

Marguerite felt an odd reluctance to join the game. She looked at the dark trees looming above her, at the black outline of the shrubbery, and felt even more uneasy. Seeing Myra linger, she went back to her. "Are you going to play?" she asked.

To Marguerite's disappointment, Myra answered eagerly, "I do want to play, only I am a little scared of the darkness. Perhaps we could hide together?"

"We could," Marguerite agreed. Joining hands, they ran toward the group gathered around Gaston, who was explaining that the big oak growing on the edge of the lawn was home. "Anyone who is discovered but avoids the seeker, runs to the tree and touches it, is a winner. Now I am going to close my eyes and count to ten." Walking to the oak, he turned his back.

"Hide!" Ada called out. Everybody scampered off.

"Where?" Myra whispered to Marguerite.

"This will do." Marguerite led her companion behind a clump of bushes. It was not the best hiding place; the old gardener seldom bothered to sweep away the dead leaves and the girls found themselves standing knee-deep in them. But at least they could see the lantern hanging on the terrace and that was a comfort.

They were the first ones to be found, but they managed to reach the oak before Gaston could catch them. Pachette was the victim; she giggled so much that she could not run. Then it was Lily's turn, and she caught Annette.

The game was becoming more and more animated. Gaston rushed around and growled, "I am a dragon. I am going to catch a fair maiden and eat her up." Giggles answered him, accompanied by a light patter of feet.

Laughter rippled out; Ada was caught.

The gaiety around her made Marguerite forget her fears. When Myra suggested they hide in a small recess under the terrace steps, she answered boldly, "Very well, you hide in there. I am going to hide somewhere else. It will be more fun."

But where? Marguerite had only a few seconds to find a good place. Ada was counting, *one, two, three.* . . . She tiptoed across the grass and stood behind the oak, just a foot away from Ada.

. . . *seven, eight, nine, ten!* Marguerite peered from behind the trunk. It looked as if Myra were going to be discovered. Ada was moving in her direction. Suddenly, she stopped and pounced. There was a slight shriek and Marguerite saw Irina slip under Ada's outstretched hand and dart toward "home."

Marguerite suddenly felt uneasy. There was something frightening in Ada's dark figure, closing softly and silently on Irina like a bird of prey. Watching from behind the tree trunk, Marguerite saw Ada's fingers touch Irina's shoulder, but the latter backed away, swung around, and ran into the dark wall of bushes growing by the west side of the house. A scream rang out, and there was a sound of someone falling.

Only a moment passed before the other players surged up, calling out, "What was it? Who screamed?"

Ada was standing still, pointing at the bushes. "Over there. Irina ran over there and then she screamed. Something must have happened to her."

Before she had finished, Gaston tore up the terrace steps and snatched the lantern off the hook over the front door. Nicolas ran behind him, dragging his bad foot. Erast and his sisters followed.

Holding the lantern high with one hand, Gaston thrust the bushes aside and said, "Please stand back. This looks like a cellar."

Standing on tiptoe, Marguerite saw the splintered remains of a wooden trapdoor.

Myra said in a tight little voice. "She must have stepped on that door and the rotten wood caved in. She may have been killed."

Malvina raised her voice, covering Annette's sobs. "It is a cellar for rakes and other gardening equipment, but it has not been used for such a long time I forgot it existed."

Gaston thrust the lantern at Erast and began to tear off the remaining boards with his bare hands. A steep flight of stone steps appeared in the circle of light. Without a word, he stepped through the opening and vanished in the shadows.

Nicolas roared in the direction of the house, "Lavrentii! Bring more light."

The trembling halo of light carried in Lavrentii's hand was getting close when Gaston appeared on the top step, Irina in his arms. "She is unconscious," he said, stepping through the bushes. But Irina began to struggle and he had to put her down.

Swaying a little, she caught at his sleeve. "It is nothing," she murmured, "I can walk."

"Are you hurt?" Vanda asked anxiously.

Irina looked at her dazedly. "Hurt? No, I don't think so. Only my hands. I grazed them against those steps, and my knees too. I wanted to call for help, but I got so frightened when the ground gave in under me, I just couldn't. I—I . . ." She covered her face with her hands and began to sob. "I was afraid. I did not want Ada to catch me. That is why I ran. I was afraid of her."

Malvina said, "Please calm yourself, Irina. You are upset and you don't know what you are saying."

But Irina would not stop. "I was afraid of her!" she screamed. "I am telling you, I was afraid."

Lavrentii raised his lantern. Ada's face swam out of the darkness, bloodless, her lips trembling.

She is going to break down and cry, Marguerite decided, but Ada's jaw was already tightening and when she spoke her voice was brittle but assured. "I am sorry for whatever I did that frightened you, Irina. I only wish you would have simply called out you did not want to play anymore. It would have prevented this accident."

Irina was beyond answering. She was wiping her eyes with her sleeve.

Malvina began, "Only peasant women—" but was stopped by her sister's reproachful glance. Looking over the girls' heads to where Erast was hovering, she ordered, "Erast, please get a jar of acacia honey from the pantry, and take it to the kitchen." Taking Irina's arm, she said, "Honey, especially the acacia kind, mixed with hot water is very comforting. You are going to drink some right away and then go to bed."

Lily asked, "Do we all have to go inside? It is such a lovely night and it is still early. We could play some more."

Malvina snapped, "Certainly not. I am sorry I permitted this silly game!"

As they all walked across the terrace, Mademoiselle, still asleep in her chair, stirred. "Is that you, Yani? Hasn't Olga caught you yet?"

Nicolas, limping along behind the girls, chuckled softly.

14

In the Attic

It took the girls a long time to quiet down after the excitement of hide-and-seek. They flitted into each other's rooms, whispered, and flitted out again the minute Mademoiselle Vanda or Ada appeared.

The last candle was scarcely blown out when the storm began. Thunder seemed to roll across the roof; lightning zigzagged across the windowpanes. The frightened pupils gathered in Irina's room because it was the largest. Myra was praying. The twins perched themselves at the foot of Irina's bed. Annette was crying and Pachette implored her to stop.

Marguerite shared a deep armchair with Lily, who took advantage of every lull in the storm to whisper, "Who was Yani? And Olga? Did they all live at Astrovo? I have a feeling you know about them. Do you?"

"Hush! You will wake Irina," Marguerite whispered back.

But Lily was insistent and finally, Marguerite told her Yani's story.

It was still raining the next morning and the gray, rainy days continued for almost a week.

Servants ran all over putting pails and basins under the leaky spots in the roof. Every evening Lavrentii lit the fire in the library to dispel the dampness that settled over the house. Everybody gathered around the fireplace. The girls talked, told stories, or played charades and forfeits.

Gaston was in great demand, especially for charades, and he organized amusing little comedies around a given word.

"But we have practically nothing to dress with," Pachette complained, trailing behind her a red tablecloth to represent a royal mantle.

Lily said, "This is such an old house. There simply must be old clothes somewhere that nobody really needs."

"Let's ask Mademoiselle Malvina," Myra suggested.

Lily frowned. "Keep your voice down. She has been in a nasty temper all this week and will probably say no. I would much rather look around for myself."

Gaston offered to join forces. "I am excellent at picking locks," he assured Lily. "A real burglar!"

Irina seemed to have completely forgotten her scene with Ada. "I am sure she did not mean to frighten me. I was just being silly," she had declared. Now she edged her way closer and asked curiously, "Where are you going to look first?"

Marguerite did not hear the answer because Pachette was calling to her to sing a duet.

Next day, in the middle of a rainy afternoon, she was alone in her room studying a mythology lesson when there was a knock at the door. Pachette burst in. "Marguerite, come quickly! We are all in the attic. Your brother and Lily found two big trunks full of old-fashioned clothes."

Marguerite jumped up and followed Pachette along the corridor toward the narrow door near the landing. "I thought it was always locked," she remarked.

"It was, but Lily found a bunch of old keys in the pantry. Your brother oiled them and one fitted." Pachette pushed the door open.

"Oh! Who is that?" Marguerite exclaimed, staring at a blond girl in a pink brocade with enormous panniers standing at the top of the stairs.

The pink girl laughed. "Don't you recognize me?"

"Annette!" Marguerite gasped. "If you had not spoken I would never have recognized you."

The attic was not as dark as she had expected; light came from several dormer windows. Boxes, trunks, and old furniture were piled high in every corner. Two big trunks stood near the stairway, their lids open. Myra was bending over one of the trunks, clutching something blue and gauzy. "I would love to try this gown on, but I dare not. Suppose Mademoiselle Malvina gets angry at us. Oh, dear! I don't know what to do. . . ."

Lily, dressed in heavy green silk with a standing collar and gold embroidery, was admiring herself in a small cracked mirror. "What nonsense! I am sure she won't mind."

Marguerite rather agreed with Myra, but the beautiful clothes fascinated her. Going to the nearest trunk, she took out an orange-and-silver brocade gown, wondering vaguely where she had seen it before.

"God be with us. . . ."

The girls turned around. Lavrentii stood at the top of the

staircase, his small, faded eyes staring at the gown in Marguerite's hands.

"You young giddy-heads!" he shouted angrily. "Let things rest in peace. Stop digging in those trunks or you may dig up more than you bargained for."

The girls looked at each other, frightened by the butler's anger. "I told you we should have asked permission," Myra murmured.

Lily recovered first. "This is none of your business, Lavrentii."

Lavrentii would not be intimidated. "None of my business, eh? I've been in this house longer than you, young lady, and I could tell you a thing or two. . . ."

Gaston suddenly appeared from behind a Japanese screen, clad in a blue jacket with an enormous lace jabot, and a yellowed wig on his head.

"May I introduce myself, the Marquis de Carabas," he announced with a sweeping bow.

At this sight, Lavrentii became even angrier. He opened his mouth but suddenly choked and, turning around, shuffled down the steps.

"What is this? What are you all doing in the attic?" Ada asked, mounting the stairway with light steps.

She gazed with surprise at Annette and Lily in their fancy attire, then at the piles of clothing on the floor. "Oh, I never knew we had such beautiful things up here." Bending over one of the trunks, she began to rummage through it.

"Be careful, Mademoiselle Ada," Gaston warned. "Lavrentii has just told us that terrible things are lurking inside those trunks."

She shook her head. "I am not afraid, and I see something

lovely there at the bottom. I think it is velvet and—" She stopped abruptly and straightened up.

Irina was coming slowly across the dusty floor.

Oh, why did she put on that gown? Marguerite thought.

The yellow gown of heavy brocade cast a sallow tinge on Irina's white skin. The big panniers made her hips even wider and the tight waist seemed to be bursting at the seams. Blissfully unaware of the effect she was producing, she called, "Here I am at last! It took me a long time to get into this gown."

She moved closer and waved her hand. There was a sound of ripping fabric, and a gap appeared under her right arm.

Ada began to laugh. Lily giggled, looked at Marguerite, and stopped. Irina gasped and tried to close the hole with her fingers.

Ada stopped laughing as abruptly as she had begun. Tossing her head, she said, "You should never have put on that gown. Don't you realize you can't wear anything like that? A sarafan would be much more becoming."

This allusion to the peasants' garb made the other girls blink. Irina said slowly, "Yes, you are right. I can see now that this gown is not for me."

Gaston stepped forward. "I agree with you," he said, his voice hard. "Mademoiselle Irina is far too beautiful to wear that ugly gown."

Ada's dark eyelashes fluttered. Pachette whispered, "Mademoiselle Malvina," and everybody stood rigid.

Malvina, followed by her sister, was negotiating the last step of the stairway. "I thought I heard voices up here," she said. "Ah, I see. . . ." She looked with amusement at the open trunks and the scattered garments.

Myra began, "We are sorry—" but Malvina waved her aside. "There is no need to apologize, Myra. I am glad these old clothes diverted you on this rainy day." She paused, and then went on, ignoring her sister's frantic whispers. "In fact, this gives me an idea. I was planning to give a ball sometime in August. We could make it a fancy-dress occasion. It would be more interesting."

Vanda said, "But Malvina, that orange-and-silver gown is the same one that . . ."

Malvina continued, "I am going to have these clothes aired and you may each choose whatever you wish to wear. I am sure we can find something for you too, Count," she added. "I must say, you look very dashing in that wig."

Gaston, his face somber, only bowed in her direction.

"I don't like it. I don't like it at all," Vanda lamented, following her sister down the stairway.

Gaston held out his arm to Irina. "May I? The steps are rather steep and your gown is so long."

That same evening, Marguerite was practicing her music in the drawing room when Gaston walked in. "That ball. Is everybody supposed to wear those old rags from the attic or are there going to be other costumes?"

Marguerite raised her eyes from the keyboard. "What other costumes?"

"You know what I mean . . . gypsies, nuns, knights in armor."

"Yes, I am sure that the guests will be dressed in all kinds of costumes."

"Hmmm, that is good. By the way, when is the messenger from grandmaman due to arrive?"

"Any day, I suppose. It is almost a week since we heard from her."

Gaston nodded curtly and left the room.

15

The Eve of Saint Ivan

After almost two weeks of constant rain, the sky finally cleared.
At the same time it became bitterly cold. Gusts of wind shook
the wobbly tiles on the roof and whistled around the corners.

"It could be November," Vanda complained, wrapping herself in a shawl and moving her chair out of the draft.

The Astrov family and the pupils were gathered around the
fireplace in the library. Gaston was not present. He had suddenly remembered his entrance examination at the university,
and he was closeted in his room.

"November?" Mademoiselle asked. "Already?"

"No, no, Mademoiselle, Vanda merely said it is so cold it
could be November instead of June," Malvina explained.

"June the twenty-third to be exact," Nicolas remarked lazily.
"The eve of Saint Ivan. Tonight, according to the charming
tale Mademoiselle Irina told us, the ferns bloom and whoever
picks the flower can find gold, or diamonds . . . rubies too,
maybe. . . ." He raised his glass of heated wine and watched it
glow in the light of the fire.

Irina laughed. "That is right, and I wouldn't mind going to that brook where we saw the ferns and trying my luck. I would need a spade for digging. The treasure is always buried in earthenware pots."

"How thrilling!" the twins chorused. "Would you really go, Irina?"

"Not in this weather."

Vanda put down the wool she was winding and sighed. "Ah, what it is to be young! Always ready for adventures! I remember how my fiancé and I—"

Erast looked anxiously at the dark windows. "I hope this terrible wind won't overturn my glass hive. It is lighter than the wooden ones."

Malvina raised her head. "I am more concerned the wind does not take the roof away." She went back to her figures.

Myra nudged Marguerite. "Those buried jewels are worth a great deal of money, aren't they?" she asked.

"I should think so!" Lily exclaimed. "My stepmother has a small ruby necklace. It is not even beautiful, yet my father says it is worth a small fortune. I wish I had enough courage to go and look for that fiery flower Irina talks about." Marguerite smiled. "Why do you have to look so superior, Marguerite? I like that story about the fiery fern."

"I do too," Marguerite answered. "But it is only a story, and you all seem to believe in it."

Ada looked up from her needlework. "I agree with you, Marguerite," she said in her best teacher's voice. "It is a legend, but you must not forget that every legend has a grain of truth in it."

"That is correct," Malvina said.

Marguerite was inclined to argue the point, but in another minute Lavrentii appeared with a tray holding what Lily called "the good-night chocolate." Soon afterward, the pupils, with candles in their hands, went upstairs.

At first Marguerite slept soundly, but the constant rattling of windowpanes finally woke her up. Then another sound came, of steps passing her door. Sitting up in bed, Marguerite thought about Lily's story of how someone invisible had passed her. But there was nothing mysterious about these steps. They merely sounded as if someone was trying to be very quiet.

Marguerite slipped out of bed. She found her slippers and threw on a wrapper. Opening her bedroom door, she peered out. The corridor was deserted. At the same time, she heard steps again, descending the stairway.

Who could it be? Marguerite ran along the corridor to the landing and peered down over the banisters. But it was too dark to see anything, and she was too late anyway. The latch clicked, the front door opened and closed. Whoever it was had gone out into the storm.

Hurrying back to her room, Marguerite lit her candle. The little tongue of flame vacillated in the draft. Marguerite noticed drops of water clinging to the window. It was raining again. Who would venture out in such weather? She remembered the conversation about the blooming ferns and Irina's nonchalant, "I wouldn't mind trying."

Tiptoeing to Irina's door, Marguerite knocked softly. There was no answer. She turned the handle gently, opened the door a crack, and listened. Peaceful breathing came from the direction of the bed. Marguerite closed the door again. It was not Irina then, but who?

Suddenly she knew the answer. Myra, of course! She could see the girl's strained face as she asked if buried treasures were valuable. Harassed by the thought that her family desperately needed money, she had gone to the brook. . . .

Marguerite fled down the corridor to Myra's room. She was so sure it would be empty, she entered without knocking and, lifting her candle, looked around. The bed had not been slept in.

Marguerite whirled around and ran out of the room. As she went down the stairs she could hear the wind getting stronger. The rain was now lashing the windows. Poor Myra, alone in the night. Marguerite stopped at the front door and saw that it was unlatched.

Marguerite was not sure which one of the doors in the long dark corridor was Malvina's. The girls hardly ever entered the family wing. But there was a ray of light under one door and Marguerite decided to try it. The door opened and she saw Malvina in a long dark robe, her hair full of paper curlers. "Myra is missing. I think she has gone to the brook."

Malvina changed color, but recovered quickly, asked Marguerite a few questions, then went to wake Erast.

In another ten minutes, both Erast and Lavrentii were in the hall, armed with lanterns.

"You can start," Malvina told the men. "I will follow you as soon as I get my cloak and pack up some bandages."

Marguerite was going to ask if she could come too, but changed her mind and decided to keep quiet. Instead, she rushed to her room and began to throw on her clothes.

Cloaked and hooded, she returned to the hall but found it empty. She knew that Malvina could not have gone far, and, pushing open the front door, she ran onto the terrace and down the steps toward the dark line of trees that marked the beginning of the park. Malvina's lantern glimmered in the distance. Marguerite ran to catch up. "I wanted to come with you. I could not sleep anyway, worrying about Myra," she panted when she finally overtook the older woman. She waited anxiously for the answer.

"I would not have allowed you to come, but I don't want you to return alone, so you might as well stay with me."

They walked on, following the gleam of the lanterns ahead of them. The wind abated slightly, but the rain was still strong, making the bottom of Marguerite's cloak cling to her legs.

Malvina said, "Vanda is going to put a hot brick into Myra's bed and prepare one of her tisanes. I told her to wake up Ada, so she could help."

"Myra started a good twenty minutes before we did," Marguerite ventured. "Perhaps she has already been to the brook and is coming back."

"I doubt it. No one could get safely down the ravine after all those rains. You will see for yourself."

The discussion was closed. They sloshed along, side by side. The lantern in Malvina's hand picked out the long tree roots extending almost the whole width of the path. Branches heavy with water hung low over their heads. Marguerite felt her feet getting colder and wetter with every step.

"Careful!" Malvina said suddenly, and Marguerite realized that they were at the edge of the ravine. When her eyes had adjusted to the darkness, she saw with horror that the ravine was flooded. Constant rains had turned the small brook into a river. The silhouettes of Erast and Lavrentii appeared and vanished again in the halo made by their lantern.

Malvina and Marguerite followed the men a few feet down the steep path and stopped. It was not possible for them to go any farther. Water was already licking at their shoes.

A few minutes passed, then Erast's voice came from below. "She is here!"

Raising her lantern, Malvina peered down. "They have found her."

Following her gaze, Marguerite saw a big boulder rising above the swirling waters, and a slight figure crouching on it. The two men, both almost hip-deep in water, were trying to take her off. Twice the current almost swept them off their feet, but Erast pressed his knee against the boulder and lifting Myra in his arms, slung her over his shoulder. Moving slowly, he began to wade out, Lavrentii lighting up the way.

"She is alive, isn't she?" Marguerite asked.

Malvina turned her head sharply. "Of course!" She began to climb up the path, calling over her shoulder, "Bring her to that big tree, Erast."

Myra opened her eyes and tried to sit up as soon as Erast laid her on his cloak.

"I did not expect that there would be so much water," she murmured. "I took a step and suddenly I was in up to my waist. I tried to get out, but the current was too strong. I managed somehow to climb on that boulder, but my fingers were getting numb. I could not hold on anymore. . . . I felt myself slipping. . . . Ah, my shoulder hurts!"

"Let me see." Malvina knelt down beside Myra. "Give me some light," she ordered Marguerite, "and you, Lavrentii, hand me that bag."

Holding the lantern and trying to steady her shaking hand, Marguerite saw that Myra's left sleeve was soaked in blood.

Taking a pair of scissors from the bag, Malvina cut through the sleeve. "Just a deep cut. Bandages, please, Lavrentii." With deft movements, she began to dress the wound.

The walk home was a nightmare. At last, the house came in sight. The front door stood wide open and the two maids hovered on the terrace steps. At the sight of Myra on the stretcher improvised from Erast's cloak, Vanda pressed her hand to her mouth. "Heaven be with us! Is she—"

"Myra is not even badly hurt," Malvina interrupted, "so there is no need for hysterics. She did lose some blood and that cold water did not help. Is everything ready in her room, the way I told you? Where is Ada?"

Vanda's little hands fluttered. "Ada? She is resting. She fainted when she heard that Myra had gone to the brook."

16

The Turquoise Ring

Myra spent two days in bed. Her shoulder was not too painful, but she looked sad and embarrassed.

"I know it was silly of me to go to that brook," she told the other girls. "But when Ada said there is truth in every legend and Mademoiselle Malvina agreed, I thought I should go and try to find a blooming fern. The money would help Papa pay his debts. Only there was no fiery fern. . . ."

At the mention of Ada's name, Lily gave Marguerite a quick glance. "It's strange Ada should have said that."

Marguerite did not want to discuss the matter, so she only said, "I really don't know," and walked away. Inwardly she agreed, and expected Ada to tell Myra she had not really meant what she'd said. The older girl did come to Myra's room, demure and quiet as usual, but she only asked about Myra's health and did not say a word more.

The girls were absorbed in their preparations for the fancy-dress ball. Piles of clothes were brought downstairs by the maids. From the twins' room came sounds of arguments as to who was going to wear what. Lily had appropriated the most elaborate of the gowns, gold brocade with enormous panniers worn over an emerald-green silk skirt with gold embroidery. After much hesitation, Marguerite selected a simple gown of some light, pale-blue material, with a tiny waist, an open neckline edged with white ruching, and very modest panniers. The sash was a little frayed at the ends but she could easily repair it. Vanda, who was the chief adviser, approved her choice. "It is a daytime gown," she said, "but you will look charming in it, and we will try and find a snood for your hair that matches the blue."

Irina was the only one who did not seem to take any interest in the costumes. She fingered the silks and lace, but refused to try anything on. "Later, there is plenty of time," she said.

One day, Marguerite found her in the library laboriously printing something on a sheet of paper.

"I am writing home." She put down her quill and shook the sand box over the fresh ink. "It takes a long time to print."

Marguerite's eyes opened wide. "You *print* your letters?"

"I have to. Mamasha can read only print. Here, this is dry now." She folded the letter and held a stick of sealing wax over a candle. Gaston entered. He looked at the letter in Irina's hand and grinned. She giggled and nodded.

Feeling rather left out, Marguerite was about to leave when Irina rose and with a hasty "I must give this to Lavrentii. He is going to the coach station tomorrow," ran out.

Going to the nearest bookcase, Gaston glanced at the rows of books as if reading the titles. "Still working on your costume, sister?"

"There is still some tucking in and hemming to do," Marguerite answered. "What about you? Did you select what to wear?"

He frowned. "No, not yet. Just anything from those trunks. One costume is as good as another." He drummed his finger on the glass of the bookcase. "I had better go and study for a while." He left the room.

He was promptly replaced by Annette, who was holding a bedraggled-looking spray of artificial roses in her hand. "I need something to wear in my hair," she complained. "I found these among my own things, but they don't go with my gown. Myra needs a fan, but she cannot afford to buy one."

"I know," Marguerite said sympathetically. "I offered her my white ivory one, but it looks too new."

Apparently rumors of the girls' complaints reached Malvina, because the very next afternoon she made an announcement.

"I hear that you all need fans, ribbons, and other things to complete your costumes. Fortunately, I was able to find the trunk containing all these things. It was tucked behind some boxes in the linen room. Are you all ready? Follow me, please."

Marguerite had never seen the linen room at Astrovo. It was located between the largest pantry and the laundry room, both out of bounds for the pupils. It proved to be not very different from the one in her grandmother's house, only the long shelves were bare instead of being stocked with piles of linen, the long tables held no baskets full of linen to be mended, and there were no irons heating on the low stove at the end of the room. In the middle of the floor stood a trunk, its lid open.

"Select whatever you need, mesdemoiselles," Malvina told the pupils. She had barely left the room when the trunk was surrounded by the eager ring of girls, digging up scarves, fans, and gloves.

"I thought this feather would go with my costume, but somehow it looks silly on me," Pachette declared, touching a pale gold ostrich feather in her hair.

"Wear it on the side, not in front," Ada suggested. "Let me show you." She plucked the feather off Pachette and put it in her hair.

"Why, it looks beautiful on you!"

"Try this shawl. It matches the feather." Myra held out a shimmering shawl.

Ada wrapped the shawl around her shoulders. "I think this goes with it too," she said, picking up a small amber necklace from the table.

Gaston, who had followed the girls to the linen room, stepped forward. "May I, please?" He assisted Ada with the clasp.

"I wish I could look so queenly," Pachette said. She held up a pair of long white kid gloves. "Oh, what is that? There is something hard wedged in one finger."

"Turn it inside out and see," Lily suggested.

"Whatever it is, is deep down." Pachette struggled with the long fingers of the glove. "Here, I have it! Oh, it is a ring!" She held up a small gold ring set with a turquoise.

Annette began to giggle. "You couldn't possibly wear it, unless your little finger fits it."

"But Mademoiselle Ada could," Myra said. "Her fingers are so slender."

"I suggest," Gaston announced, "that Mademoiselle Ada sit on that chair." He indicated the only one in the room. "I shall go on one knee and present the ring to her as becomes a royal subject."

Ada blushed. An almost childish expression of pleasure crossed her face.

"What is this?" Irina, who had been at the other end of the long table, strode up and took the ring off Pachette's palm.

"Pretty." She turned the ring around and held the stone to

the light. Then she put the ring on her little finger. "Ouch, it hurts," she complained, pushing the ring over the first joint. "I did not realize it was so small. I had better take it off." But when she tried, the ring was stuck.

"What am I going to do now?" she cried, staring at her hand.

"Try soap," Marguerite advised.

Other girls crowded around Irina, each suggesting her own remedy. At last Vanda, attracted by the commotion, came in and promptly sent Annette to the kitchen for some oil. "Butter sticks, but oil makes things glide."

Oil was brought and the ring came off immediately. Irina went to wash her hands. Gaston, his spirits revived, picked up the ring and turned to Ada. "Now we can present to our queen—"

She cut him short. "We have wasted enough time already. Come, mesdemoiselles, we are forgetting that we are supposed to have a German lesson at this hour."

Her voice had an undertone of anger, but Marguerite thought she could also detect a quiver of tears.

Gaston stood twirling the ring in his hand.

Marguerite was just going to take it from him when Mademoiselle wandered into the room. At the sight of the ring, her faded eyes opened wide. "Little Yani's ring. Alexander gave it to her, but she had to keep it hidden so that Olga wouldn't know. Are you going to put it on her finger and tell everybody she is your bride?" Coming closer, she peered at Gaston. "Oh, but you are not Alexander! And Yani is dead, isn't she? They are all dead. . . ." Holding out her hands, she pleaded, "Take me to my room, please. I feel so tired."

"I shall be honored, Mademoiselle." Gaston took the old lady's arm and led her out. As she was following them, Marguerite heard Ada whisper, "They are *not* dead." A chill ran down Marguerite's back.

Ada's voice haunted Marguerite all through the rest of the day, reminding her of Yani's voice calling Alexander, of the figure in the library window, the strange steps in the corridor, the parrot screaming. She slept fitfully and when she got up the next morning, she felt so tense her hands shook, making her drop the long strips of cloth and paper she used for curlers.

A sudden whiff of smoke made her cough. She looked around, wondering where it came from. It was seeping from under the door. Pressing her hand to her mouth, she ran into the corridor.

Clouds of smoke were pouring from Irina's room. Marguerite's eyes burned. She brushed at them with her hand, then stepped back quickly as Ada rushed past her screaming, "No! No!"

At the same time, Irina tumbled through the smoke. Her hair was singed and one of the wide sleeves of her peignoir was burned around the edges, the lace hanging in dark wisps. She was sobbing. "Someone did it. Someone tried to burn me. I know I did not spill any spirits on that tray." Behind her, barely visible through the smoke, was Myra, a pitcher in her hand.

Suddenly, the corridor seemed to be full of people. Vanda pushed her way through, asking anxiously, "What has happened?"

"Irina spilled some spirits while heating up her curling irons and it caught fire," Lily began.

Irina interrupted her. "I did not spill anything and I was not even curling my hair at that time. I was only going to. But when I tried to light my lamp, I realized the tray was swimming with spirits. Only it was too late. The whole thing went up in flames, right into my face." She touched her singed hair. "Then Myra rushed in with some water and poured it over the tray." She gave a long sob. "I could have been burned alive!"

Craning her neck, Marguerite peeked into Irina's room. On the dressing table a small spirit lamp was standing on a metal tray, all blackened with soot. A pair of curling irons lay nearby. There was a big black spot on the rug and on the bottom of the carved mirror frame. The tassel of the draperies on the nearest window was charred, too.

Pachette came running. "I found Mademoiselle Malvina and she is coming," she reported breathlessly.

Malvina's sharp heels already could be heard mounting the steps. "Where is the fire?" she asked calmly, approaching the girls. "It could not have been a very serious one. How did it start? Pachette said something about Irina's spirit lamp spilling over."

"It did not!" Irina cried wildly. "And the fire may not have been big enough to burn the house down, but I could have been. If you don't believe me, look at my hair." She put up her hand and stared with horror at the long charred lock. "It was done on purpose," she murmured, while tears began to run down her face. "I know it was done on purpose to disfigure me, maybe even leave me blind."

"Gracious!" Vanda whispered, pressing her hands to her chest. "What is she saying!"

"She does not know herself what she is saying," Malvina answered.

Marguerite knew that Irina's upsets never lasted long. She stepped forward. "May I take Irina to my room, mademoiselle? I am sure I could arrange her hair so that the burned part would not show. That might make her feel better."

126

Malvina looked relieved. "An excellent idea. Thank you, Marguerite."

Irina did not protest. She followed Marguerite and fell into the nearest armchair. "It is dreadful! I must look like a scarecrow."

Marguerite wiped Irina's face and hands with toilet water and began to work on her hair, trimming off the singed strands and rolling the rest into neat curls. Irina began to calm down and soon recovered sufficiently to talk.

"Do you think Mademoiselle Malvina is very angry with me? Could she send me home?"

"For having a spirit lamp and curling irons in your room? No, she wouldn't do that," Marguerite assured her. "But she is probably displeased about it. Why don't you use curlers like the rest of us?"

"Because those rags and papers give me a headache. No, I meant for my screaming that someone had spilled the spirits on purpose."

"She knows you were upset. Do you really think so?"

Irina thought for a moment. "I don't really know. I did at first, but now I wonder. . . . I am so big and clumsy. Perhaps I did tip that lamp and it spilled. Besides, who would do a terrible thing like that? No, it is just not possible. No one would be that evil."

"But wouldn't you rather go home?" Marguerite asked, trying to choose her words carefully. "After all, you would be . . . safer."

Irina began to laugh. "Safer? With Papasha raging about my wasting his five hundred rubles? Oh, no!" A mischievous sparkle danced in her eyes. "No, I really couldn't leave. I simply *must* be here for the ball."

17

Before the Ball

"Is *that* the costume you are going to wear at the ball?" Marguerite looked doubtfully at the faded orange jacket with silver embroidery hanging over a chair in her brother's room.

Gaston, perched on the windowsill, raised his eyebrows. "Do you object?"

"I do. It is too old."

"Certainly it is old. That is the whole point. We are going to re-create history, bring back the glory of the past."

Marguerite examined the lace cuffs. "These should be taken off and washed. Look how soiled they are. The lace should be mended; it is torn in several places. Goodness! There are two buttons missing. Surely you could find something better in all those trunks upstairs?"

"Yes, yes, but everything is too big for me."

"If you selected something nice, we could make it fit. Both maids are good seamstresses and I could help."

"Don't bother. This one will do perfectly."

"Irina is not taking any interest in her costume either." Marguerite was irked. "She chose a purple brocade that was probably worn by some old lady. It does not suit her at all."

"Really? Well, it is for her to decide what to wear. To change the subject, is grandmaman's messenger coming tomorrow or Friday?"

"Tomorrow probably. He usually comes on Thursdays. Why do you look so anxious? Are you expecting any special news from grandmaman?"

"No, nothing special." Gaston bit his lip, as if to hide a smile.

He must have been up very early the next morning, because when Marguerite woke up before seven, there was a letter from her grandmother stuck under the door.

Taking the letter to bed, Marguerite read it avidly. Her grandmother wrote that there were no more cases of smallpox. The rains and thunderstorms had caused some damage to the orchards, so there was less jam making and pickling than usual. *Maybe just as well,* the countess wrote. *I am getting too old to run around the house, supervising the staff and making sure everything is done properly. I must confess I feel lonely as well and I am simply longing to see you again, dearest child. I see from your letters that you are enjoying the companionship of the other pupils and that your studies are of value to you. However, I am not quite sure you are really happy at Astrovo. Some happenings you mention in your letters seem rather strange, but I cannot decide whether those are facts or you girls are simply scaring each other. One thing I must make quite clear to you. If you are frightened or even uneasy, you don't have to wait until October. Come home with your brother in August. Decide for yourself. I shall be, of course, only too happy to see you.*

Marguerite put the letter down and clasped her hands in

relief. Of course she was going home with Gaston. It did not need any thinking over. She would insist they start the day after the ball—no, a day later. It would be too tiring to get up early. Picking up the letter again, she read the few remaining lines. *I hope you are learning some good music. I look forward to your playing to me in the evenings while I knit.*

Marguerite felt guilty. She had forgotten to learn the exercise Ada had set for her and she had a music lesson that very afternoon. Now there was no time. She only hoped Ada would not make scathing remarks.

She found out that there was no need to worry. Ada accepted her apologies with a light "I am afraid we all lost our heads in the preparation for the ball. You will learn it for the next lesson." She paused. "Are you doing some sewing for your brother as well?"

"I wish I were," Marguerite answered. "His costume needs repairing, but he would not let me touch it."

"Oh?" Ada began to turn the pages of some music on top of the piano. "What color is his costume?"

"Orange and silver," Marguerite answered.

"What a coincidence! Mine is orange and silver too."

It was on the tip of Marguerite's tongue to say, "Really? I thought it was red," but some instinct told her to keep quiet.

Still leafing through the music sheets, Ada continued, "Since we don't have to bother about that exercise, Marguerite, let's have a singing lesson instead. I have just found a little lullaby. It is very old-fashioned, but the melody is beautiful and simple at the same time." She placed the music on the piano rack and sat down beside Marguerite. "We shall try it together. Or no, perhaps I should sing it to you first."

She struck a chord and began to sing, *"The sun has gone down and the sky is full of stars. I shall rock the cradle softly—"*

She stopped abruptly, her hands poised above the piano keys. In the sudden silence a young, lilting voice sang, *"—and each star a tale shall tell."*

Marguerite looked over her shoulder. The big drawing room was empty. "Someone is in the library?" she suggested, half-rising from her seat. "Shall I look?"

"No, don't bother. You won't find anyone there, and I don't care. No, I don't care! I have been afraid for too long; there is no more fear left in me." Throwing back her head, she called defiantly in the direction of the library door, "You want to sing a duet with me? Very well, so we shall!"

She started to play again. *"Sleep my baby, sleep,"* the two voices sang, blending together.

Marguerite felt as if she were engulfed in some terrifying nightmare.

A shrill, discordant note cut the air. Ada covered her face with her hands. "I can't live like this any longer. I can't . . . I can't. . . ."

Marguerite sat still, longing to put her arms around Ada, but uncertain whether the older girl would like it.

Ada settled the question. "I think we shall postpone our singing lesson till tomorrow." Her voice still shook. "I would like to be alone now." As Marguerite rose to go, she said with an effort, "Please don't mention this . . . incident to anyone. My Aunt Malvina could be right. This house is full of echoes."

Anxious to escape, Marguerite answered, "I am sure that she is right," and fled across the hall, out onto the terrace, and from there to the green shelter of the big oak. Sitting down on the circular bench, she pressed her cheek against the trunk and felt comforted. The oak was so tall, so strong and somehow reassuring. Little by little, her calm returned. There was really nothing she could do, she told herself. Ada had asked her not to tell anyone what had just happened in the drawing room. This meant she could not go to her brother and insist they leave immediately, which had been her first thought. And after all, it could have been an echo. . . .

The sun was pleasant. Marguerite folded her hands in her lap and tried not to think anymore, but just enjoy the soft breeze and balmy air.

From the corner of her eye she watched Malvina come out of the house, a wide-brimmed straw hat on her head, a long gray apron around her waist. Armed with pruning shears, she began to trim the lilac branches broken by the storm. In spite of her dislike toward the older woman, Marguerite could not help noticing how tenderly she handled every spray. She recalled how she had one day seen Malvina pick up a baby swallow that had fallen out of the nest and place it back. Was she doing it out of kindness, or only because the flowers and the swallow were part of Astrovo? Marguerite could not decide. One thing was clear, however. It would be better for her not to let Malvina see her. She might ask some awkward question. Pupils were not supposed to sit outside during lesson time. Moving softly, Marguerite slipped through the side door and joined the other girls who were doing needlework under Vanda's supervision.

The next lesson was French literature. To Marguerite's surprise Ada appeared, with dark circles under her eyes, but otherwise cold and reserved as usual.

Evening came, and the girls gathered in the drawing room. At first Marguerite was reluctant to enter, but the chattering and laughter around her soon made her forget the strange voice singing the lullaby.

Gaston sauntered in. He just could not bear sitting alone in his room with the boring books. Perhaps they could play parlor games to give a rest to his poor head.

Pachette proposed forfeits, and even Ada joined in. Unrestrained by their elders, the girls threw themselves wholeheartedly into the game. Even Lily forgot to look bored as she sat opposite Gaston. "You have just received one hundred rubles. You can buy what you want, but do not buy black or white, do not say yes or no. What would you buy?"

"A new top hat," Gaston answered promptly.

"How nice," Lily simpered. "It will be bright pink, I suppose?"

"No!" he screamed, outraged.

Everybody called out, "Forfeit! Forfeit!"

To pay his forfeit, Gaston was ordered to hop across the room on one leg, which he did with alacrity.

Soon everyone had a forfeit. Pachette was made to improvise a solo dance, her sister to multiply seventeen by seventeen in her head, and Lily to recite three lines from El Cid backward. Ada held out longer than anyone else, never buying black or white and never saying yes or no, but in the end she got caught too, deftly trapped by Gaston, and was condemned to turn around ten times, whirling swiftly like a top. She collapsed giggling onto a chair.

The game over, everybody settled down to rest. The girls were talking about their costumes and Gaston was leafing through an album of old engravings.

Ada moved restlessly in her seat, then said to Gaston, "Your sister told me that your costume is in orange and silver. It so happens that mine is in the same colors."

"Er . . . yes. That is right," Gaston muttered.

Ada went on with a smile, "I thought that perhaps we could

open the ball together, since our costumes are so similar."

Gaston became completely disconcerted. He started to say something, broke off, and looked pleadingly at Irina. She looked back at him, shook her head, and suddenly broke into peals of laughter.

Ada frowned. Around them, the babel of voices became hushed, then died down altogether.

Ada turned to Irina. "May I ask just what is so amusing?"

Irina stopped laughing, looked at Gaston, and promptly started again, hiding her face behind her sleeve.

Getting up, Ada marched across to Irina. "I have told you again and again not to use that peasant gesture. But apparently when one is born a peasant, one remains a peasant, and you have just proved it."

Gaston tried to intervene. "Mademoiselle Ada, please, it is only . . ."

Irina ignored him. Her blue eyes angry, she asked, "So only peasants can laugh?"

"It depends what one is laughing at."

"Well, then I shall explain." Irina threw back her head and looked Ada full in the face. "I was laughing at *you.*"

For a moment, Ada did not seem to understand; then red spots flamed on her cheeks and she came a step closer. "How dare you? You miserable little upstart. I will make you sorry for this."

Raising her hand, she was about to strike, when Vanda rushed in and caught her niece's arm. "Ada!"

The color slowly faded from Ada's face. "I am sorry, Aunt Vanda."

Gaston jumped up. "It was only a misunderstanding, Mademoiselle Vanda. I am afraid I provoked this er . . . unpleasantness and—"

Vanda would not listen. "Yes, yes, I am sure it was only a misunderstanding. I think we are all tired and should retire a little earlier than usual. Good night, Count."

Gaston took the hint and disappeared. Marguerite dashed out of the room and caught up with him in the hall. "Wait!" she gasped, clutching at his sleeve. "Explain to me just what made Irina laugh like that. There must be a reason." She studied her brother's face. "Gaston, are you and Irina planning some mischief to spring on us at the ball?"

A guilty look crossed her brother's face, but he recovered promptly. "Really, Marguerite, you are becoming annoying. I simply did not expect Mademoiselle Ada to suggest we open the ball together. I suppose I looked surprised and Irina, I mean Mademoiselle Irina, thought it funny." He frowned. "Actually, I *should* open the ball with her since she is the daughter of the house. Well, it can be arranged. . . ."

"See!" Marguerite cried. "You are planning something! Do tell me about it."

But Gaston suddenly became angry. "Look here. Leave me alone and attend to your own business." He began striding away, but turned around. "I can promise you one thing. Irina is going to be the belle of the ball."

Marguerite did not answer. Fighting back tears, she went to her room. When she finally did drop off to sleep, it was not for long. Every few hours she would wake up, roused by a strident parrot's voice, screaming, "She is ugly! Ugly! Ugly!"

18

The Garden by Moonlight

Preparations for the ball began early in the morning. The two maids were kept running from room to room as the pupils tried on their finished costumes and clamored for a stitch here or a tuck there.

Lily was furious because the shoes sent to her from home did not quite match her green gown. "It is all my stepmother's doing," she raged. "I sent a sample. Just look at it—" She showed each girl in turn a small piece of green silk. "And now look at these. They are a different green!" She kicked viciously at the pair of high-heeled brocade shoes.

Myra pulled Marguerite aside. "Do you think anyone would notice if I wore cotton stockings instead of silk ones? I hoped I could save enough of my allowance to buy a pair, but I couldn't."

"It may not be too noticeable in the evening," Marguerite answered evasively, thinking that Myra's costume left her legs visible almost to the knee. The simple short-sleeved gown suited Myra; it was a pity the effect would be spoiled.

She was wondering whether her stockings would be too small for Myra when Irina suddenly appeared. "I heard you needed silk stockings. Here, take these." She pressed a pair into Myra's hands.

"Oh, thank you, Irina! But can you really spare these? Do you have others to wear yourself?"

Irina dismissed the question. "I haven't looked. But I won't need these anyway." She went to her room, her shoulders shaking with laughter.

Marguerite stared after her, then ran downstairs. A few minutes later, she was standing in her brother's room. His costume was in the same place, the cuffs still soiled, the jabot unpressed. He can't possibly wear it tonight, she decided, feeling faintly alarmed.

Going slowly back to her room, she noticed that preparations for the ball were going on downstairs as well as in the girls' quarters. Apparently help had been summoned from the village, for two women were on their knees, cleaning the rug in the drawing room. The double door leading to the ballroom was open, exposing the polished parquet floor. Lavrentii was working on the furniture while women brought in a stack of wax candles and proceeded to place them in the sconces on the walls.

On the landing, Marguerite almost collided with Pachette. "Have you seen? It is raining! If the roads get too muddy, the guests won't come. Then what shall we do? Dance with each other?"

Marguerite glanced out of the narrow landing window. "It is only a drizzle so far. Perhaps it won't affect the roads."

She proved to be right. By noon even the drizzle had stopped, leaving a light fog lingering above the ground.

Dinner was served early and immediately afterward the pupils were sent to their rooms to get dressed.

Lily quickly took possession of one maid and the twins appropriated the other. After waiting for a while, Marguerite gave up and began to dress herself. She struggled into her starched petticoats and began to put on the pale blue gown, when she noticed that a side seam on the skirt was becoming unstitched. She quickly reached for her workbasket, but she had no more blue silk left.

Throwing on a wrapper, Marguerite went to knock at Irina's door. A startled voice said something. Taking this for permission to enter, Marguerite opened the door and walked in.

Irina was standing with her back to her dressing table, her hands spread over the top of it.

"Blue silk thread?" she replied. "I may have some in there. Take whatever you need." She nodded in the direction of a sewing basket standing on the windowsill.

It took Marguerite time to extricate the blue skein from the jumble of spools, scissors, and tape.

"I hope you don't mind my taking all of it," she said. "There are only a few threads left."

"Of course not. Just take it," Irina answered, and pressed herself even closer to the dressing table.

What is the matter with her? Marguerite wondered. Vanda had promised to come to her room at six o'clock to do her hair, so she hurried out.

She was just in time. Vanda appeared a few minutes later, wrapped in a trailing pink peignoir.

"We don't have to powder your hair, my dear," she told Marguerite, seating her in front of the mirror. "Yours is a daytime gown. We will simply brush your hair up and tie it with this blue ribbon, leaving the ends to fall like streamers.

We will leave these two bunches of curls to frame your face. Here! You are ready! Isn't it becoming? I must go to Lily now. Her gown calls for powdered hair, which takes some time. Luckily, Ada has decided to do her own hair."

"And Irina?" Marguerite asked, thinking how awkward Irina was when it came to hairdressing. "Her purple brocade is an evening gown."

"Oh, she is not going to wear it," Vanda answered lightly, gathering her combs and brushes. "She said she had selected something else that does not need a special hairdo."

"She never mentioned anything about wearing another costume." But Vanda was already gone.

For a second, Marguerite felt tempted to ask Irina just what gown she was going to wear and why she was being so secretive about it. Before she could go, there was a knock on her door and Myra burst in. She was already dressed in her diaphanous tunic, but her hair was hanging loose instead of being tied in a Greek knot at the nape of her neck.

"Did you see it?" She closed the door behind her.

"See what?"

"Come!" Seizing Marguerite's arm, Myra led her to the window. "I was dressing and just happened to glance out to see if the weather was getting better, and I saw— Oh!" She sprang back, covering her mouth with her hand. "It is still there. Look!"

Marguerite peered into the deepening twilight. The sky was still cloudy but some moonlight was seeping through. Something white attracted Marguerite's attention. It looked like a statue. She strained her eyes . . . yes, it was a statue rising above a nest of greenery. Farther on there was another one. The moonlight became stronger. Now she could distinguish several flower beds and the outline of an arch made of climbing roses.

"It can't be. It is a dream."

"Not if we both can see it," Myra answered.

"Perhaps it is only the moonlight. . . ."

"It could be," Myra agreed eagerly. "It does change things. . . ." Her words trailed off and she shivered.

"Are you still dressing, Marguerite?" Pachette called from the corridor. "May I come in and show you my shepherdess costume?" She danced in, curtsying and pirouetting.

"You look charming!" Marguerite admired the pink-and-white sprigged panniers worn over a short skirt in deeper pink. On Pachette's head was a wide-brimmed straw bonnet with long silk streamers, and she was holding a beribboned staff in her hand.

"Where is your sister?" Myra asked. "She is dressed as a shepherdess too, I believe."

"Yes, but her costume is all yellow. She wanted to be a shepherd, but Mademoiselle Malvina would not let her. She has forgotten to sew ribbons on her staff, so she is doing it now."

"Are we supposed to go downstairs at the same time and make a grand entrance?" Myra asked. She kept glancing in the direction of the window.

"We don't have to," Pachette answered, smoothing her skirt. "Mademoiselle Malvina simply said that those who are ready first could come downstairs to help her welcome the guests. Goodness, it is almost eight! I must run and see how Annette is doing."

Myra followed her, walking slowly and averting her eyes from the window.

Left alone, Marguerite hurriedly finished dressing. With shaking hands, she adjusted the small black-velvet mask and pulled on her long white gloves.

She closed the door of her room behind her. The sudden

longing to be with other people, to talk to them, to lose herself in the crowd, was so overwhelming that she almost ran along the corridor toward the stairway.

She had barely reached the landing when she felt a breath of air, and at the same time she smelled the scent she knew only too well now. She stopped and listened. Yes, someone was descending in front of her. She could hear the *tap, tap* of small sharp heels.

Gathering all her courage, Marguerite dashed forward, intent on seeing the person who was in front of her. She rounded the curve of the stairway and slowed down. There was no one to be seen.

Clutching tightly at the banisters, Marguerite somehow reached the hall. It was deserted, but a faint hum of voices was coming through the half-opened doors of the big ballroom.

Before Marguerite had time to take another step, the ballroom doors opened wider and Lily tumbled through, wild-eyed and shaking all over.

Marguerite gazed past Lily into the deserted ballroom beyond.

Lily nodded knowingly. "So you heard them too? I was so sure everybody was assembled already, I walked straight in. I even heard music."

"The musicians are in the servants' hall and are probably tuning their instruments. That is what you heard, Lily," Malvina's voice said behind the girls. She was not costumed, but was wearing a long, wine-red gown embroidered with seed pearls around the wide neckline. A spray of diamonds shone in her graying hair.

Smoothing her long gloves, she went on in a slightly reproving tone, "You girls have too vivid imaginations. Your companions are dressing and chattering upstairs and their rooms are just above the ballroom. No wonder one can hear their voices through the floor." She forced a smile. "Our guests seem to be arriving. I can see carriage lamps outside. Where is Lavrentii? He should be here to announce the names."

In another moment everything was normal. Lavrentii appeared and announced the first guests, a stout lady in yellow silk and her three daughters costumed as a violet, a daisy, and a poppy.

Standing on either side of Malvina, Lily and Marguerite greeted the guests and were presented to them. There were bows, curtsies, and more bows. Lavrentii grew hoarse announcing names.

The big reception at Astrovo had officially begun.

19

The Ball

Marguerite's terror slowly ebbed away as she sat in the ballroom with Myra and looked at the costumes. A demure nun was walking with a mushroom. A tall oak kept catching at the window draperies with branches of greenery that were attached to his arms. An angel lost one of her wings and was led away by Vanda to be patched up.

Vanda herself was dressed as a fairy, all in pink, a wand in her hand. Marguerite was trying to guess how she had achieved the intricate hairdo of small curls piled high and topped with a small silver crown when she felt Myra's hand on her arm.

"Look." Myra nodded at the nearest window.

Marguerite raised her eyes. She could see the tall blooms of white roses.

There were no roses in the garden. Marguerite's fears returned.

The arrival of Nicolas, dressed as a magician in long black robes and a pointed hat, distracted the two girls. He was followed by Erast in some strange green attire. It took Marguerite some time to realize he was supposed to be a grasshopper.

Ada was among the last to appear. She was pale and kept biting her lower lip.

Gaston was nowhere to be seen.

Soon the ballroom was full. Kings, monks, dashing knights, dairymaids, and princesses drifted from one group to the other, talked, laughed, and tried to guess who was hiding under the black masks.

The musicians slipped through the side door. One took his place at the piano, two violinists and a flutist sat on chairs nearby. Marguerite watched them settle down and put their music on the racks. The man at the piano took a gold coin out of his pocket and showed it to the other three, who nodded and produced similar coins from their pockets. The flutist shook his head. "A merry young man!"

Young man? Marguerite repeated to herself.

"I must go and look for my brother," she told Myra, just as the clock struck eight.

The pianist's hands fell on the keys. A crashing chord swept the ballroom. The doors leading to the hall opened wide and Gaston appeared, Irina on his arm.

Both were dressed in Russian national costumes; not the brightly colored peasant attire, but the rich garments of the boyars, the old Russian nobility.

Irina's sleeveless blue sarafan was of a heavy, gold-threaded material and matched the kokoshnik, embroidered with pearls and gold, that crowned her braided hair. Her hair gleamed softly under the white veil that fell to her shoulders. She was nervous. Marguerite could see the wide-sleeved white blouse under the sarafan move quickly up and down.

Gaston, made taller by his long kaftan, high fur cap, and soft red boots, looked so unlike himself that Marguerite did not recognize him at first.

A whisper of admiration passed across the ballroom. The handsome couple reached the center of the floor and began to dance. It was not a lively peasant dance, but a solemn courting by a nobleman, trying to win his bride-to-be. Gaston advanced, Irina retreated, infinitely graceful in every movement. Slowly, the tempo quickened and the dance became more passionate. Finally the young couple were dancing hand in hand.

The music stopped at last and the ballroom rocked with applause. Gaston led Irina to a seat where she was immediately surrounded by her companions and the guests. The musicians began to play a polonaise, which usually opened a ball. Gaston bowed in front of Ada. She drew back. "I am already engaged."

Behind Marguerite, Lily giggled. "She is vexed and no wonder. Your brother paid her back for having been so nasty to Irina."

Not vexed, *hurt*, Marguerite thought. I wonder if Gaston realizes, or if he thinks it is simply a good joke.

A quadrille followed the polonaise, then a gavotte. Marguerite executed all the steps mechanically. The gavotte ended and strains of a waltz filled the ballroom. A knight in armor asked Marguerite to dance. As they waltzed, Marguerite became aware that there were not many couples around them. The waltz was still considered a new and somewhat wicked dance. The girls sitting by the wall and pouting behind their fans were probably forbidden by their mamas to dance it.

Gaston and Irina glided past. Marguerite heard him whisper, "Courage! Courage! Let me turn you around now. Left foot forward. Very good!"

Another couple came close. Marguerite caught sight of Ada's set lips.

It was beginning to get very hot in the ballroom. The smell of melting wax candles became mixed with the smell of perfumes and flowers.

Marguerite's partner looked at her with concern. "You look tired, mademoiselle. Would you permit me to take you onto the terrace for a breath of air?"

Marguerite shrank back. To go outside among all those strange statues and flowers? But the next minute her courage returned. "Why not? It is a very warm night and the roses smell wonderful." She looked at the white roses nodding behind the windowpane. The knight followed her gaze. "Roses, mademoiselle? I did not see any as we drove through the grounds. It is a pity everything is so decayed. My father remembers the time when Astrovo was one of the most beautiful estates in these parts."

He could not see the roses then. Yet Marguerite was sure that Lavrentii, circulating with a tray of refreshments, was aware of something mysterious. He shot frightened glances at every window he passed.

Trying to keep her tone light, she said, "Perhaps I should stay inside. It might be too damp on the terrace after the rain."

The knight did not insist and as the dance ended, he escorted her to a seat. The minute he vanished in the crowd, Marguerite got up and slipped into the library to rest a little.

It was pleasant to find the library deserted, lit only by an oil lamp and two candelabras on the mantelpiece. Feeling a few stray wisps of hair, Marguerite went to the mirror over the fireplace.

As she looked, her eyes widened. Instead of the walls of tall bookcases, the mirror reflected a white, sculptured arch and a vast room beyond with a mullioned window at the end. A crystal chandelier lit up the walls covered with pale blue silk. Graceful chairs and love seats, all upholstered in white, were grouped around a spinet. On top lay a violin. A harp stood nearby. A tall rack held a sheet of music.

Taking a deep breath, Marguerite looked over her shoulder. The library was as usual—rows of dusty books, worn-out leather chairs, the big oak table. She remembered Lavrentii saying that there had once been a music room, but that it was destroyed by the fire. Maybe the story had stayed in her memory. With an effort, Marguerite made herself turn to the mirror again.

The music room was still there, but it was no longer deserted. A young man in an orange-and-silver jacket was standing by the spinet with a girl in a blue brocade dress. The girl was not pretty, but the small round face was eager and sensitive, and the eyes danced with childlike gaiety.

Marguerite recognized the couple immediately. She had seen them both before on the night she and her brother came to Astrovo.

Taking off her long white gloves, the girl put them on a chair and began to rearrange the turquoise ornaments in her powdered hair. The young man watched her. Coming close to the girl, he said something. At least, his lips moved. Marguerite could not hear a sound. The girl evidently did; she blushed and the white glove she had just picked up fluttered onto the rug. The young man retrieved it and made a movement to help the girl put it on, but instead he took her small hand and raised it to his lips.

Fascinated, Marguerite kept staring into the mirror. It seemed to her that she actually was standing in that music room of the past. A door opened and a dark-haired girl in an orange-and-silver gown stepped in. Marguerite shrank back at the hate in the black eyes. The girl's slender fingers seized the ivory fan hanging at her belt, bent it, and began to break it to pieces.

Marguerite heard no sound, but the young man abruptly turned around and faced the intruder. Suddenly, the image in the mirror faded and the dark library came back into view.

Marguerite collapsed into the nearest chair and covered her face with her hands. "It was Alexander," she whispered, "and Yani. Olga surprised them. But it all happened so long ago. How could I see them now? Yet I am not afraid. I am more afraid of something that seems to be coming. . . ."

She was just going to get up when someone came in. Gaston! And Irina.

"I told you the waltz is easier than many other dances," her brother was saying.

Irina laughed. "Only when I dance it with you. I always feel safe when I am with you."

"I am happy you feel that way." There was a strange catch in Gaston's voice that Marguerite had never heard before. "And I am happy that this room has not been invaded by other people, that it is dimly lit and . . . that we are together."

Marguerite realized she could not be seen behind the high back of the armchair. Sinking deeper into the big chair, she held her breath, hoping they would not discover her. Craning her neck, she saw that they were standing by the fireplace.

Gaston was looking at the window. "Strange, how the grounds look different tonight. Perhaps it is a trick of moonlight, but I see statues and flowers."

"Where?" Irina turned her head. "Heaven be with us!" she whispered, crossing herself. "That is devil's work."

"Please don't be afraid. You know that I will never let anything bad happen to you."

"I am not afraid, and you know why. . . ."

Gaston took Irina in his arms.

It was only Marguerite who heard the door open, and only

Marguerite who saw Ada standing on the threshold, her gaze fixed at the mirror that reflected two faces merged in a long kiss.

The door closed softly. Ada was gone. Marguerite thought, She does not resemble Olga much, yet just now she looked exactly like her. It was the hate in Ada's eyes that made her resemble her grandmother.

Marguerite slipped noiselessly out of the library. It was strange to find the ball still going on, everybody dancing and gay. At midnight, the masks were taken off to the accompaniment of laughter and exclamations. Lavrentii announced supper, and Marguerite let herself be escorted to the table by a young toreador.

After supper a farandole began. All the dancers joined hands and ran through the ballroom and the drawing room, across the hall, up one stairway, and down the other one. For a second, Marguerite found herself swept away by the fun of it, but it did not last. Heavy foreboding seized her again and stayed, chilling her heart.

20

The Past Recalled

It did not surprise Marguerite to find Gaston on the terrace early the next morning. Looking gay and more flippant than usual, he was sitting on the balustrade and flicking his boots with a small willow branch.

"You sly little thing!" he greeted Marguerite. "I saw you slip out of the library last night."

She did not return his smile. "Yes, I happened to be there when you came in. A little later someone else entered and saw you and Irina."

He raised his eyebrows. "Who? One of the guests?"

"No, Ada."

"Ada? That was unfortunate, but never mind. Do you think she was vexed about the Russian dance?"

In Marguerite's opinion *vexed* was not the right word to describe Ada's feelings, but she felt too tired and listless to argue. She asked instead, "How did you come to think about that dance?"

Her brother's face cleared. "Just an inspiration! I wanted to show Ada how beautiful Irina could look and I knew that an old Russian costume would suit her perfectly. I told her about my idea and she thought it would be fun. So she wrote to her mother and asked her to find a costume somewhere. I wrote the same to grandmaman. Later we decided to do a dance. It was really awkward when Ada asked me to open the ball with her, but I managed to bribe the musicians and we had our dance *before* the ball—something like a prelude." He began to laugh. "It was such fun to see all those people gape when we danced. I was a little uneasy about Mademoiselle Malvina, but she was quite amiable about the whole thing. As to Ada seeing me and Irina in the library—well, I am free to marry whom I like."

"Marry? You asked Irina to marry you?"

"Not yet, I mean not officially. I intend to write to grandmaman first and make sure she welcomes Irina into the family. It will be almost a week until the messenger comes, so I have arranged for one of the stableboys to ride over and give the letter to her. I will pay him well, naturally. Not that I doubt for a minute that grandmaman will give us her blessing. Did she not always say we were both free to choose our spouses?"

Marguerite did not answer. Gaston went on, "We will have to wait, of course. I still want to go to Heidelberg and finish my education. No use pretending I want to settle in the country and spend my life growing wheat or apples. I am planning to go into diplomatic service and this will require more studying. But once we are engaged, I think—"

"Alexander!"

Marguerite clenched her hands. Never before had she heard Yani so close.

Gaston looked around. "I can't see anyone. . . ."

Marguerite swallowed hard. "No," she said firmly, "You

can't see anyone, but they are here, Yani and Alexander. I told you about them."

"Yes, yes . . . I believe you." Gaston put an arm around her shoulders. "Why don't you go and have some more rest. Your companions will probably all sleep till noon. In the meantime, I promise you that in my letter to grandmaman, I will ask her to send a coach for us this coming Monday. Only three days to wait. . . . And then we will be safely back home."

"What about Irina?"

"As soon as I receive an answer from grandmaman, I shall go to her parents and ask for her hand. I shall also insist they take her away from here. Now, go and rest."

Marguerite was already in her room when another pitiful call came from outside, accompanied by a heartrending dog's howl.

Clapping her fingers to her ears, Marguerite huddled in an armchair, sobbing. "I wish we were going home *now*, this very minute, this very minute. . . ."

At last, exhausted by crying, she let her head fall against the cushioned back of the chair. In another moment she was fast asleep.

Two loud voices arguing just outside her door woke her up. She looked at her clock. She had only slept for a few hours. The clock showed eleven. Sitting up, she listened to the argument raging in the corridor. Lily and Malvina, she thought.

"I keep telling you I was wide awake!" Lily screamed. "How could I sleep with all those carriage wheels rumbling right underneath my window? I knew that everybody had left hours ago. So I got up, went to the landing, and looked down into the hall."

She paused for breath and Malvina asked, "And just what did you see in the pitch darkness? I put the lamp and the candles out myself before retiring."

"It was not dark. That old Venetian lantern on the ceiling was alight. I know it was, because that is what I saw first, the red and green and blue reflections on the walls."

Malvina's tone became even more sarcastic. "How very interesting. Especially since that lantern has not been lit for at least thirty years."

"It *was* lit, and I saw"—Lily's voice sank almost to a whisper— "I saw people, all dressed in old-fashioned clothes like those we found in the attic. They were taking leave of each other. A footman kept coming up and announcing something—I could not hear what he said, but I suppose he was announcing that the coaches were at the door. That was strange. . . ." She paused. "All the time I looked, I could not hear a sound, yet I *know* that those people were talking."

Marguerite rose and opened her door. Lily stood just outside, facing Malvina. The latter was saying, "What a vivid dream. I suppose you agree that this was all a dream, my dear? In fact, you don't seem to be awake right now. I suggest you lie down again. There will be no classes today."

"I don't care whether there are classes or not!" Lily screamed. "I am writing to my father to come and fetch me. I am not staying in this house any longer."

"As you wish, my dear, but you do realize that this will mean living with your stepmother," Malvina answered.

Lily's lips quivered. She was obviously making every effort not to cry. Other girls emerged from their bedrooms, clutching their peignoirs around them.

"Well, what do you want to say now?" Malvina asked, as Lily stood biting her lip.

Before she had time to answer, Pachette cried, "I want to say something. I heard what Lily was telling you, Mademoiselle Malvina, and I believe her. I saw something strange myself last night. I was passing through the library after supper and I hap-

pened to glance at the mirror to see if my petticoat was show-
ing. I saw a different room in the mirror, not the library. The
walls were of pale blue silk, and a dark-haired girl was playing
a harp. While I was looking, it all faded away."

"Another vivid dream!"

Pachette stood firm. "It was not a dream, but I am not going
to argue about it. I am doing like Lily, writing to Papa and
asking him to take us home."

"But sister, Papa said we cannot have our debut until we
learn French and other things." Annette put a hand on
Pachette's shoulder.

Pachette shook her off. "You stay if you want to. I am sending my letter with the next mail."

Malvina looked around. "Does anyone else want to leave?"

Marguerite did not answer. Myra murmured, "I wish I
could." Irina just shrugged.

"I only want you all to know," Malvina went on evenly, "that
the mail is not going to the coach station till next week. I trust
that by that time you will all have changed your minds about
leaving, and will not disturb your relatives with such vagaries."
Turning her back on the girls, she went toward the stairway,
past Ada's closed door.

Left alone, the pupils stood silent, avoiding looking at each
other. Then Irina yawned and announced she was going back
to bed. The others followed her example, Lily muttering about
leaving regardless of the consequences.

A sketchy meal, consisting mainly of the reheated remains of
the festive supper, was served at three.

"Is it lunch or dinner?" Pachette whispered to Marguerite
with a giggle.

"Let's call it a repast." Nicolas installed himself at the end of the table. "I miss a few familiar faces? Do you know anything about it, Niece Ada?"

Ada looked desperately tired, with enormous shadows under her eyes. "My aunts are having trays in their rooms. Uncle Erast left for Tula to pay some bills."

"Ah, yes." Nicolas nodded. "I heard Malvina talk to him about it this noon. I understand she even paid a visit to the apiary. So we are actually paying our bills!" He raised his shaggy white eyebrows. "What an intoxicating new experience! Oh, here is our handsome young man."

Gaston had just slipped into the dining room. "I was writing a letter and forgot the time," he explained.

"A love letter, no doubt?" Nicolas teased.

"Uh—I suppose you could call it that. Actually, it was to my grandmaman, but. . . ." He looked at Irina across the table. The girl blushed furiously and looked down at her plate.

Ada's mouth tightened. Turning to Myra, she said sharply, "I am sorry you don't like your food, but you must realize that the cook is old and worn out after preparing the supper last night."

"I did not say anything about not liking my food," Myra answered in a trembling voice. "I can't eat because—because I am afraid of something and I don't know what it is."

Ada's color rose. "If you don't know, then there is no need for this scene." She turned away.

The meal ended in complete silence. Immediately afterward everybody began to drift away.

Lily said, loudly enough to ensure that Ada could hear, "I am going to get one of the maids to pack for me. This way I shall be ready when Papa comes."

"Could you send her to us when she is finished with your things?" Pachette asked, ignoring her sister's whisperings.

Left alone, Marguerite wandered into the library. From the

drawing room came the sound of the piano. Irina was practicing and humming to herself. Gaston had disappeared. Marguerite was annoyed. She wanted to ask him whether he had actually managed to send the letter through the stableboy.

The music in the drawing room stopped, and Marguerite wondered whether Gaston was with Irina. But a few minutes later, she saw him going past the library window. She made a movement to call him, but her attention was distracted by the sight of an embroidery frame standing by the window. It was her task, assigned by Vanda: a spray of wild flowers in needle-point.

It suddenly occurred to Marguerite that it would be awkward to remove the unfinished embroidery from the frame to take home with her. There was very little left to do, just a few small leaves here and there. She could finish them now.

Sitting down, Marguerite drew the embroidery frame toward her.

21

In the Apiary Again

The house was very quiet. It seemed to Marguerite that she was the only one awake. Tilting the frame toward the light, she examined the embroidery. She would need a different shade of green for the remaining leaves, she decided, so they would all look different, like real leaves.

She glanced at the window where a branch was swaying against the sky. Only . . . the leaves were not green. They were withered and yellow, tinged with red. Just as on that day, Marguerite thought, when she went alone to the apiary. Perhaps, if she did not watch them, they would disappear, like the white roses on the night of the ball. . . . She rose, almost upsetting the embroidery frame, and went across the room, trying not to run.

She had just reached the hall when Lily came in through the door leading to the terrace. She seemed to be highly amused about something.

At the sight of Marguerite, she exploded into giggles. "It is so funny. . . ."

"What is funny?" Marguerite asked.

Lily took a handkerchief out of her pocket and began to fan herself with it. "I went to the pantry to get some fruit—I needed it after the meal we had—and I met Irina just leaving through the back door. She said Mademoiselle Malvina had lost a ring this morning somewhere in the apiary. She asked Irina to look for it."

"Did she go?"

"Oh, yes. You know how good-natured Irina is. She could never refuse. But listen to what happened next." Lily began to giggle again. "I did not find any fruit, so I went out of the back door and walked around the house, just because I had nothing else to do. And guess whom I met! Your brother! He was on the terrace, about to go for a stroll."

"And then?" Marguerite asked.

Lily half-closed her eyes. "Well, I told him that Irina was in the apiary and waiting for him. I made it sound mysterious. He fairly flew down the terrace steps. Now those two will be together without a chaperon, since Monsieur Erast is in Tula. Won't they enjoy themselves! Perhaps they will kiss."

"Hush!" Marguerite interrupted. "Listen!"

A slight hiss came from the old grandfather clock standing in a recess under the stairway. It had broken down years ago and was never repaired, Vanda had once told Marguerite. Now the hands were moving. As the girls watched, the hissing came again and the clock slowly boomed four times.

"Alexander!" A heavy smell of decaying leaves seeped into the hall.

Lily blanched. "What was it?"

Marguerite did not hear her. She was seeing herself on the terrace, with Lavrentii on the steps, telling her the story of Yani and her lover. *It was a damp autumn day, and the fallen leaves smelled something terrible. . . .* That was the day young Alexander went to his death past the music-room window. Yani saw him and wanted to call him, but she never did. Now she, Marguerite, had done exactly the same thing. But the tree with the wasps' nest was gone, she reminded herself—and remembered the bees in the glass hive at the apiary. Something dreadful was going to happen there. There was no use reasoning with herself. She knew with a strange certainty that her brother was in danger, and Irina too. When had she seen him? Five minutes ago? No, ten was more likely. If she ran hard, really hard, perhaps she could overtake him.

Marguerite whirled around and ran across the hall, onto the terrace, and into the garden.

Abruptly she stopped, trying to decide whether to take the shortcut along the apiary avenue, or to go across the park. Lily had said that Irina went out through the back door, but Marguerite doubted she would venture to take the apiary avenue. No, she must have gone across the park, and if Gaston wanted to overtake her, he would go the same way. This would give Marguerite a chance to reach the apiary first by using the shortcut.

But suppose there is nothing wrong in the apiary? she asked herself, hurrying toward the vegetable garden. She could never explain to Gaston that strange, overwhelming feeling of approaching disaster.

Slowing her steps, she passed through the garden, dense with the pungent smell of aromatic herbs. Shall I turn back? she asked herself. The sun is shining, everything is green. I could have imagined that smell of decaying leaves.

But a minute later it came again, heavy, penetrating, reminding Marguerite of gray November days. It was not only the smell; yellow leaves crunched under her footsteps and the breeze sent them raining on Marguerite's shoulders. They stuck in her uncovered hair and clung to her skirt. The sun was gone; clouds floated low over the bare trees.

Shivering, Marguerite stopped and looked around. She saw a dark figure running toward her. Marguerite recognized the woman she and her companions had once seen on the road. But then they saw her at a distance. Now she passed quite close, her black dress flapping around her legs, a bunch of keys swinging at her belt. Her mouth was open as if she were screaming, and she kept pointing at something over her shoulder.

Now Marguerite *knew:* her brother and Irina *were* in danger.

She dashed forward and stopped again. Was this the apiary avenue? Now the abandoned barns seemed to be full of stock. Marguerite could hear the mooing of cows and the voices of dairymaids calling to each other. The neighing of several horses came from the stables, and from farther away the cackling of fowl.

Marguerite started to run again. Exotic flowers gleamed through the glass of the greenhouse as she ran past it. A groom exercising a horse appeared, and vanished again behind the outbuildings. Somewhere a harmonica began to play and a hoarse voice sang.

Marguerite ran on. She was just rounding a bend when a group of men came from the opposite direction. They were carrying something between them, something long, covered with a gray cloak.

Marguerite knew it was the body of Alexander.

Stifling a scream, she swerved and clung to a tree trunk while they passed. As soon as they had vanished, she drew a long breath and started to run again, stumbling on the overgrown tree roots, falling, picking herself up, and running again. A prickly branch caught her hair, and she tore herself free. Then she saw Gaston with Irina.

They must have met in the park and were now cutting across the meadows instead of taking the road. They were too far away to hear her call. She had little hope of reaching the apiary before they did, but still she went on running, ignoring the pains in her chest and side.

Slowly, she was gaining distance. "Gaston!" Marguerite put all her strength into the call, but neither her brother nor Irina seemed to have heard. They were now close to the hedge surrounding the apiary. They were closer. . . . They were at the gate. . . . They were entering. Both were so absorbed that they forgot to close the gate behind them.

Marguerite caught sight of the big glass hive gleaming in the sun. For a brief second, she saw a tall dark figure slip behind the hive.

A sharp pain in her chest made Marguerite gasp for breath. She staggered another step and sank to the ground, just outside the apiary gate, gazing with horror at the glass hive that was tilting, shaking, and slowly leaning forward. Marguerite realized that at any moment the bees were going to escape.

Neither Gaston nor Irina paid any attention to their surroundings. They walked slowly across the grass, their heads together, her hand on his arm. The hive leaned over even more.

Ignoring the pain that was tearing her chest, Marguerite called again, "Gaston! Irina! Stop!" She had no hope that her voice would reach them.

They stopped nevertheless. From somewhere a young girl in a blue dress, followed by a shaggy dog, darted up and stood with her arms outstretched, barring their way. . . .

A split second later the hive crashed to the ground, swarms

of bees rising above it. Gaston whirled around. Snatching the peacock shawl from Irina's shoulders, he threw it away as far as he could. A cloud of bees followed it, attracted by the color. With his other arm, he caught Irina by the waist and dragged her into the thickest bushes.

Half-crouching, half-standing, Marguerite watched the familiar figure of Malvina towering over the debris of the glass hive. She seemed to be mesmerized as she gazed at the girl in blue. Then she screamed and thrust out her hands. Attracted by her movement, the bees closed upon her.

Marguerite flattened herself on the ground and covered her face with her hands.

Then the screams came, terrible, agonizing screams. Marguerite raised her head to look. The girl in blue and the dog were gone. All she could see was a black mass of bees, swarming over a body stretched on the grass.

22

The End of the Story

Sitting at her dressing table, Marguerite was sorting out trinkets and ribbons and putting them into a large flat casket on her lap. Her trunk, all packed, stood by the door, her hatbox on top of it. The old coachman and the two stableboys had spent the night riding around the countryside and delivering messages to the pupils' homes, asking the parents to come and take their daughters home.

Now it was early afternoon. The twins were already gone. Lily followed them. It was a relief to see her leave. From the moment Malvina was brought, dying, to the house, Lily kept screaming that it was her fault. She should have guessed that something strange was going on when Irina was asked to go all alone to the apiary. But instead of trying to prevent her from going, she had sent Gaston after her. If he and Irina had died, it would have been her fault. It was only when she saw her stepmother, a quiet, attractive young woman with a kind smile, that she calmed down and clung to her.

If Irina had not met Lily at the door, no one would have known that Malvina had sent her to the apiary. That was probably how it was planned, Marguerite thought, smoothing a pair of gloves.

A knock came at the door and Ada entered. Her face was so pale, it looked almost transparent. "I came to say good-bye," she said, "and I also want to talk to you. I don't care what the other pupils think of me, but you were always so understanding and then . . . there is your brother. . . . I want both of you to know that I—that even though I disliked Irina, I never tried to harm her in any way. At first I did not even realize what my aunt Malvina was trying to do. It was only after I happened to overhear Lily talk about the pepper in Irina's basket that I remembered seeing my aunt with the keys of the spice cupboard in her hand. Still, I could not really believe she wanted Irina maimed or killed."

"I did not suspect your aunt at all," Marguerite answered frankly, "and I did not think you did it either. I thought the pepper got into the basket by accident. But later . . ." She hesitated. "When Myra went to look for the flaming fern and nearly drowned, I wondered whether you fainted because you had expected *Irina's* body to be brought from the stream. And you did say there is a grain of truth in every legend."

"No, no!" Ada exclaimed. "I was going to explain what I meant. I read somewhere that people liked to bury valuables near ferns because those plants usually grow in shady places, so one could not see that the ground had been disturbed. Only my aunt never gave me the time, and then the conversation changed. Oh, I had my suspicions! So later I went to Irina's room, to make sure she would not go to the stream. But she was already fast asleep. I never dreamed Myra would go."

"I saw you run toward Irina's room on the morning that the

tray with spilled spirits flamed up," Marguerite said. "Did you suspect something was going to happen?"

"I did see my aunt slip into Irina's room the evening before," Ada answered. "But she stayed there only for a few seconds. Of course it does not take long to pour some spirits onto a tray." She shook her head. "One incident I can't explain. You remember that hide-and-seek game? I feel terribly guilty about scaring Irina so that she ran and fell into that cellar. Yes, I enjoyed scaring her, but I did not even suspect the cellar existed and I don't think Aunt Malvina knew about it either. Oh, she did have some plan for that evening. There was some reason why she approved so heartily of our playing on the grounds. We will never know what her plan was."

"Let's not talk about all this anymore," Marguerite suggested. "Your aunt Malvina is dead. Let her rest in peace."

Ada nodded. "You are right. She paid with her life for her schemes. I only wonder why she did not try to escape after she had knocked over that glass hive. Your brother and Irina escaped."

Marguerite was going to say, "Because she stood there and looked at Yani," but decided against it. Neither Gaston nor Irina had mentioned the vision. She would keep it secret too. "What do you mean by 'schemes'?"

Ada looked down. "I am sure you realized that my aunt Malvina wanted me to marry your brother. My marriage into a wealthy family like yours would have brought money for Astrovo; perhaps it could even make it as it was years ago. Irina was in the way. . . . I should have warned her. I wanted to many a time, but I was afraid of my aunt. I always was afraid of her."

"Your aunt could have sent Irina away under some pretext," Marguerite suggested.

"It would not have helped. Your brother would have followed her. My aunt knew it and . . . I knew it too."

"He possibly would." Marguerite wondered whether to tell Ada that at that very moment her brother was somewhere with Irina, asking her to be his wife.

There was a moment of silence. Ada rose to go. "There are many things I must take care of," she told Marguerite. "My aunt Vanda is asleep. It was a great shock and she is to stay in bed for a few days."

"You are not planning to leave Astrovo?" Marguerite asked.

"Oh, no. Uncle Nicolas did talk about selling the estate, but Uncle Erast would not agree. He thinks we can manage. Now that he has a free hand, he wants to try and make the orchards and the vegetable garden bring in some money. I am going to help my aunt Vanda keep the house." She glanced around. "I don't really mind staying. It seems different here . . . so peaceful, and I am not afraid any longer."

With a hasty "I shall see you again before you leave," she slipped out of the room.

Marguerite did not try to detain her. She could hear Gaston's steps coming along the corridor. From the way he entered, she guessed that something had happened between him and Irina. He asked casually, "Was it Mademoiselle Ada who just came out of here? I only saw her back."

"Yes, it was Ada." Marguerite began to tell her brother about Malvina.

He came close to Marguerite and put both his hands on her shoulders. "I think it is time for me to beg your pardon, sister. I wouldn't believe you when you were telling me about the evil in this house. I shrugged it all off as fantasies. You were right. If I had only listened to you, perhaps Irina and I would not have come so close to losing our lives in the apiary." He frowned. "Come to think of it, why did Malvina want to kill *me?*"

Marguerite thought back, trying to visualize the scene. "I

believe she did not see you," she answered at last. "Irina came first, so conspicuous in her peacock shawl, and that is when I saw Malvina run behind the hive. She probably waited for Irina to come a little closer before pushing it over. She never expected anyone to come with her."

Sitting beside the little table that was now clear of Marguerite's workbasket and her sketch album, Gaston picked up Yani's silk ball. "Talking about Irina. She is not going to marry me."

"No? Did you show her grandmaman's letter? It was so warm, so kind."

"She read it, and she was touched by it. Still, she said no."

"I don't understand," Marguerite murmured. "What were her reasons?"

Gaston let the ball roll across the table. "I will try and tell her reasons to you in her own words. When I told her I loved her, she answered, '*Are* you or *were* you in love with me?' And when I protested, saying I could not understand what she meant, she said, 'Don't you see for yourself? For the entire summer you were the only young man here with a flock of pretty girls around you. We were all having fun and you felt you just had to fall in love with one of us. First it was Ada, then me. I should have told you there and then I would not make the right wife for you. Remember how Ada laughed when I got all primped up in that brocade gown? She was right. I must have looked funny in that finery, and that is the way I would look to your grandmother and other gentlefolk, maybe even to you. Yes, I know, you got me dressed up in that old Russian costume and that suited me, but I could not go on masquerading all my life. Only . . . we did not think about all this. We were having a good time and we never cared if we hurt someone else. For Ada, it was not just fun. She really loved you. Now look how it has all ended . . . in horror and death. The girls are leaving and the summer will be soon over. So let's both go back to the lives God meant for us.' "

"And those were her last words?"

"Yes, we said good-bye to each other. Her father is coming to fetch her later this afternoon."

Getting up, he walked to the window. "I see a coach coming. Are the rest of your companions gone?"

"Lily and the twins. Myra is leaving tomorrow."

"Then it must be for us. Yes, I see our coachman. He can come up for your trunk. I shall take this." He picked up the hatbox. Marguerite put on her bonnet, and they went downstairs.

Ada was waiting for them in the hall. "Let me know sometimes about yourself." She kissed Marguerite. "I shall be quite lonely. A letter would be a great joy."

Gaston bowed to her and she curtsied. About to follow his sister, he suddenly stopped. "I am going away to Germany for two years. When I am back, may I pay you a visit?"

"I shall be waiting for you."

From somewhere in the drawing room came Mademoiselle's voice. "Where is Yani? I can't find her anywhere."

"Come, sister." Gaston took Marguerite's arm and led her through the front door. Nicolas was standing on the terrace, supported by his gold-topped cane. "I trust you have had a very educational time with us, mademoiselle," he said with his usual satyr grin.

Marguerite's trunk was already strapped to the roof of the coach. Gaston helped her in and sat down beside her. The horses moved. Marguerite scanned the depths of the garden. Mademoiselle was right. Where was Yani? Poor little Yani, who could not save herself or her lover but saved another man and another girl. No call came from behind the trees, no face lurked behind the library window; everywhere was at peace.